MONKEY BUSINESS CAN BE DANGEROUS!

I couldn't breathe. I tried to scream for help. But my voice choked inside my throat. A rope was tightening around my neck.

Someone was trying to strangle me.

My eyes popped open. I was in my bed. It was pitch dark. I grabbed at the rope around my throat. Was I dreaming?

I twisted and turned, gasping for breath. I yanked at the rope. It squeezed tighter. Suddenly I was free. I sat up and stared wildly around.

Who was trying to kill me?

I clapped a hand over my mouth to stifle a scream.

On my pillow sat the blue monkey, staring at me with one gleaming black eye.

R.L. Stine's
Ghosts of Fear Street ® #29

THE TALE OF THE BLUE MONKEY

A Parachute Press Book

A GOLD KEY PAPERBACK
Golden Books Publishing Company, Inc.
New York

A GOLD KEY Paperback Original

Golden Books Publishing Company, Inc.
888 Seventh Avenue
New York, NY 10106

Copyright © 1998 by Parachute Press, Inc.

The Tale of The Blue Monkey written by Elizabeth Winfrey

ISBN: 0-307-24902-6

First Gold Key paperback printing April 1998

10 9 8 7 6 5 4 3 2 1

Cover art by Jim Ludtke

Printed in the U.S.A.

Chapter ONE

"**S**ome of *them* used to live here," Bess whispered. She glanced from me to my brother Danny. The candlelight turned her eyes into shadowy black pools. "Right on this very spot."

"The Fear family lived in *our house*?" I gulped.

"Not exactly." Our sitter shook her head. Her soft gray bun of hair bobbed. "It was a different house, Amanda. This was long, long ago—more than fifty years. There was another house on this spot. And some of the Fears lived in it."

I shuddered. "Creepy!" The Fears were the most evil, cursed family in the history of Shadyside. Probably even in the history of the world! And they lived *here*?

That made me nervous.

"What's so creepy about that?" Danny scoffed. "This is Fear Street, after all. Where else would they live? You're such a chicken, Amanda. *Cluuck! Cluuck!* Look out! It's Amanda, the Amazing Chicken Girl!"

"I am not," I muttered. "Quit it."

Danny is twelve—a year older than me. He loves scary stories and movies. The scarier the better, he says. Even though I know for a fact that he used to sleep with a night light until he was ten. But that never stops him from making fun of me.

My dad says it's not that I'm chicken. It's just that I have a *very* good imagination. Whatever. All I know is, scary stories *terrify* me. And Bess tells the scariest stories I've ever heard.

Danny always makes her tell at least one when she comes over. He turns out all the lights in the living room and lights candles and everything. I either have to suffer through it—or listen to Danny make endless cracks about me being a chicken.

"Anyway." Bess leaned forward in her creaky rocking chair. "The Fears who lived here were not from the rich part of the family. In fact, they were very poor. They had two children—a boy and girl, just the same ages as you two. They even had red hair and freckles, like you two."

"You're kidding!" I gasped. "A family just like us— who lived just where our family lives now . . ."

Maybe we *were* that family! Maybe our destiny

was to relive whatever horrible fate happened to them in Bess's story! And maybe—

"Go on," Danny urged Bess. "Get to the good part!"

"Across the street—in the same house where the Kroncks are now—lived a famous toymaker," Bess resumed. "This toymaker made the finest dolls in the world, right there in a workshop in the house. The dolls were so beautiful that people lied and stole to get them. One man even fought a duel with someone when they bought the doll he wanted to give his daughter.

"People in Shadyside began to say the dolls were too good to be made by any ordinary toymaker. They said the Fear Street toymaker must be a powerful magician.

"The little Fear girl heard the rumors. But she didn't care if they were true or not. She only cared about the wonderful dolls that were made right across the street from her house.

"Every evening after dark, she sneaked across the street and peered into the toymaker's window. She gazed at all the dolls, wishing that she could have one—just one—for her very own."

"Dolls? Gag me!" Danny made puking sounds.

Bess ignored him. So did I. So far, this story was much less creepy than Bess's usual ones. I liked it!

"One day, the toymaker perched a monkey doll on

3

a desk right next to the window," Bess told us. "The monkey was covered with blue fur and had twinkling button eyes. Its arms seemed to be reaching out to the little Fear girl.

"She would sneak out of her house and gaze in at it every night. She longed to cradle it in her arms. To stroke its blue fur. But her family had no money to spend on dolls. She knew she could never buy the blue monkey.

"Then one night, the toymaker left the window open. The girl reached in through the open window and touched the monkey. Its blue fur was soft, just as she knew it would be.

"The girl picked up the toy monkey. Maybe she only wanted to hold it. But once it was in her arms, she couldn't put it back. She slipped it under her jacket and ran home."

"She stole the monkey?" I exclaimed. "Uh-oh!"

"What happened? Did the toymaker catch her?" Danny asked.

Bess glanced at her watch. "Oh, look at the time! If I don't get dinner started, we'll be eating at midnight."

"Wait!" I cried as Bess got up from the rocker. "Finish the story, Bess. Please!"

"I will," she promised with a smile. "*After* dinner." She turned to my brother. "Danny, I'm making your favorite tonight—deluxe burritos."

"Yes!" Danny exclaimed.

"And double chocolate chip cake for dessert, Amanda." Bess winked at me.

"Double chocolate—yum!" Chocolate is my favorite food. "And *then* the rest of the story, right?"

"Good things come to those who wait," Bess chirped. She headed down the long hallway to the kitchen.

Danny picked up the remote and clicked the TV on. "All right!" he whooped. "The Friday night movie is *Terror in the Mist!*"

Mom and Dad never let us watch horror movies. But Mom and Dad weren't home. They left Shadyside earlier that day. They travel a lot for work—they're nutrition consultants, and they do a lot of weekend workshops at spas and stuff.

Usually, when Mom and Dad go away, Danny and I stay over at friends' houses. Or at our boring aunt and uncle's house. But it was Spring Break, and everybody was away. So Mom and Dad asked Bess to stay with us. She used to babysit in the evenings when I was younger. But this was the first time she'd spent a whole weekend with us.

Bess is pretty cool. She's a great cook—especially of burritos and brownies and other things my parents never let us have. And she looks like a sweet old granny. But she knows just about every spooky story there is.

I curled up on my end of the big brown sofa,

picked up my book, and tried to ignore the TV.

Then I heard it. A slow tapping noise. It sounded as if it was coming from behind me.

I glanced irritably at Danny. Was he trying to scare me?

No. He was staring like an idiot at the TV set.

There it was again. *Tap, tap, tap.* Now it sounded as if it came from across the room.

My skin crawled. "Danny?" I whispered. "Mute the TV for a second."

Danny shook his head. "No way!"

"I heard something," I told him. "Come on. Mute it!"

Grumbling, Danny hit the mute button. We both listened.

Silence.

"I heard tapping," I insisted. "Like this." I rapped three times on the glass end table.

"Oh, that?" Danny snickered. "That's the sound the girl in *Terror In The Mist* hears right before she gets killed by the crazy axe murderer. You are such a chick—"

Tap, tap, tap.

We both froze. Danny's eyes grew wide.

It definitely came from behind us this time. I was afraid to turn around. Afraid of what I would see there, framed in the big picture window.

Finally I couldn't stand the suspense a moment longer. I whipped around.

My mouth fell open in horror.

"Aaaaaaah!" Danny shrieked.

A pale face was pressed against the glass. One wild eye glared in at us. The other was in shadow.

The horrible figure raised a hand to tap on the window again.

There was something in the hand.

Something long. And sharp. And gleaming.

"Noooo!" I screamed. "He has a knife!"

Chapter TWO

I jumped to my feet. So did Danny.

We both backed away from the window, screaming.

The horrible figure tapped on the glass again. "Hey!" he yelled. His voice came through faintly. "It's me, kids!"

Huh?

Did we know this maniac?

I took a closer look at the knife in his hand.

Wait a second. That wasn't a knife.

It was a gardening trowel.

Relief flooded through me. "Omar!" I cried.

Danny peered cautiously at the window. Then he staggered back to the couch and collapsed. His face was ghostly white.

"Omar? The gardener?" His question was barely a whisper.

"Right," I panted. I still felt breathless from fear.

Omar stared in at us with one large, blue eye. The other eye was covered with a patch. A jagged scar ran down his cheek. Bushy, white eyebrows formed a straight line across his forehead. His thin lips stretched tight across his face as he smiled.

Danny sat up. "I knew it was him," he declared. "I was just trying to freak you out, screaming and everything."

As if I would buy that!

Omar stuck out a thumb and motioned toward the front door.

"I think he wants to talk to us," Danny said.

I wasn't too psyched. Maybe Omar wasn't a knife-wielding maniac. But he still looked awfully creepy with that eyepatch and scar. And what was he doing knocking on our window at seven o'clock on a Friday night?

I didn't trust him.

But I wasn't about to tell Danny that. He'd just call me the Amazing Chicken Girl.

I followed my brother to the front door. He yanked it open. Omar stood on the front porch. He was scraping mud off the thick soles of his boots with his trowel.

"Um, hi," Danny said.

Omar just kept scraping. He had on black pants, a faded black sweatshirt, and a tattered baseball cap. He looked more like a burglar than a gardener.

"Did you want to tell us something, Omar?" I asked.

Now Omar raised his head. He stared fixedly at me with his one good eye. "Tell your dad I'm still working on that gopher problem of his." He tapped his trowel on the front porch railing to shake off the soil. "It's coming along. You tell him that."

"If Dad finds one more gopher hole in the lawn he's going to flip," Danny warned.

It was true. For the past few weeks, holes had been popping up all over the backyard. Dad was freaking out. The lawn was his pride and joy.

"You tell him," Omar said again. Then he turned and seemed to melt into the night.

Danny shut the front door. "I can't believe you were scared of Omar, Amanda," he said. "He's just an old guy."

"Me?" I snorted. "*You* screamed just as loud as I did!"

"I was faking," Danny insisted.

Bess stuck her head out of the kitchen. "Kids?" she called. "Was someone at the door?"

Unbelievable! She missed the whole thing!

"It was just Omar, the gardener," I called back. "Telling us about the gopher holes." I headed for the kitchen. "Will you tell us more of the story now?"

Bess laughed. "Oh, all right. Come on and help me with the salad and I'll keep going."

In the kitchen, Danny started washing lettuce while I made salad dressing. Bess spooned chicken and rice into burrito skins.

"The morning after the little girl took the monkey," she told us, "the toymaker came to the Fears' front door. The little girl opened the door. She was the only one home.

"'I know what you did,' the toymaker told her. 'You stole my blue monkey. You're a thief!'"

"Oh, no! Did the toymaker call the police?" I asked. "Was the little girl thrown into jail?"

Danny rolled his eyes at me. "Kids don't get thrown in jail, dummy. Especially not for stealing stupid dolls."

He thinks he's so smart. I made a face, crossing my eyes at him.

"The little girl felt awful about what she'd done," Bess continued. "She went to her room, got the monkey, and brought it to the toymaker. 'Here's your monkey,' she said, handing it over. 'I'm sorry. I didn't mean to take it.'

"The toymaker stared at the little girl for a moment, then handed the monkey back to her, saying, 'Keep it. It's a gift from me to you.'"

Bess fell silent.

"That's it?" Danny demanded after a second. "That's the end? He gives her the monkey and says have a nice life? That's lame!"

Secretly I agreed with him. It was nice that Bess told us a story with a happy ending for once. But it was pretty lame.

Then Bess spoke again.

"The little girl thanked the toymaker and hugged the monkey to her," she said in a low voice. "But that isn't the end."

"It isn't?" Danny and I both leaned forward.

"No." Bess shook her head. "Because then the toymaker broke into evil laughter and shouted, 'Hah! You took my gift! Now you are cursed forever! The monkey will bring you doom!'"

Chapter THREE

"**T**he monkey will bring you doom!"

I stared at Bess, chilled. Her voice rang with a strange, harsh note. Her face was pale.

It's as if she believes this story really happened, I thought. I shivered.

"What did the toymaker mean?" Danny demanded. "What happened to the little girl?"

Bess seemed to shake herself. "Later. I'll finish the story later," she told us. She began to assemble cake ingredients on the counter. "Now—will you two run across the street and ask the Kroncks if we can borrow a cup of cocoa? I need it for the cake." She handed Danny a measuring cup.

"It's still a lame story. I don't believe in curses," Danny declared as we walked out the door.

"Me either," I agreed.

But secretly, I wasn't so sure. Not at all.

I gazed across the street at the Kroncks' house. I wasn't wild about going over there. The same house where the evil toymaker once lived. That's what Bess said.

"Um—maybe Bess needs some sugar too," I mumbled. "I'll go back and ask her. You go ahead, Danny."

"We have a whole big bag of sugar. I saw it on the counter," Danny retorted. Then his eyes narrowed. "Wait a second. You don't want to go because the Kroncks live in the house from Bess's story. Right? You actually believe that story is true! Come on, Amanda, admit it."

"Well, it could be," I argued. "After all, this is Fear Street. You know weird things happen here. Besides, I think Mr. Kronck is creepy."

"Chicken!" Danny scoffed.

"Will you quit calling me that?" I snapped.

Danny grinned. "Then prove you're not. Come with me."

So I went. It wasn't like I had a choice, after that.

Danny knocked on the door. A second later, Mrs. Kronck's wrinkled face appeared in the small window. She peered out at us. She had to be about a million years old! A pair of wire-rimmed glasses magnified her watery eyes.

"Yes?" she said as she slowly opened the door.

"Who is it?" a gruff voice called from inside the house.

"It's only the Muller children," Mrs. Kronck answered.

I peeked around Mrs. Kronck and saw Mr. Kronck. He sat in a wheelchair, frowning. He looked mean—as usual.

"Our—our sitter Bess sent us over," I stammered. "She asked if we could borrow a cup of cocoa."

"Do you know Bess? She tells the best stories!" Danny exclaimed. "About stuff that happened here on Fear Street."

Mr. Kronck suddenly wheeled his chair to the doorway. "That woman has no right to tell those stories!" he yelled angrily.

I jumped. Danny backed up a few steps.

"No right!" Mr. Kronck cried. Then he grabbed the wheels of his chair and rolled down the hall. We heard a door slam.

I exchanged a glance with Danny. Mr. Kronck was definitely creepy!

"You'll have to excuse my husband," Mrs. Kronck quavered. "He gets a bit cranky after spending hours in the workshop."

Workshop? I thought Mr. Kronck was retired.

Maybe he had a hobby.

Like making evil toys!

"What does Mr. Kronck do in his workshop?" Danny asked.

My question exactly!

Mrs. Kronck frowned and shook her head. "You don't want to know," she said, almost to herself.

My heart jumped. *What* didn't I want to know?

"I'll get you that cocoa." Mrs. Kronck took the cup from Danny and walked toward the kitchen. Danny and I followed.

The house was dark and dusty. The floorboards squeaked under our feet.

"Great wallpaper. Nice flowers. Roses, aren't they?" I babbled to Mrs. Kronck. I do that when I get nervous. "It looks kind of like a collage. Um—is it new?"

Mrs. Kronck stopped and gave me a strange look. "That wallpaper has been in this house for more than fifty years."

Fifty years?

Bess's story supposedly took place fifty years ago. . . .

"Mr. Kronck's parents built this house," Mrs. Kronck went on. "He was born and raised here. After they died, the house was sold. But a few years ago Mr. Kronck and I heard the house was for sale again, so we bought it. We're very happy here on Fear Street. It's where we belong." She gave a little sigh. Then she said, "Wait here. I'll get that cocoa."

As she rummaged around in the kitchen, I turned to Danny. "Fear Street is where they belong?" I whispered. "Who belongs on Fear Street? Danny, these people are *weird*. And it sounds like Mr. Kronck was here fifty years ago!"

"So what?" Danny shook his head. "You think he's the toymaker?"

"Well . . ." I trailed off.

"Chicken," Danny murmured. *"Cluuck! Cluuck!"*

Somewhere in the house, I heard banging.

"Maybe that's Mr. Kronck in his workshop," Danny whispered. "Maybe he's making evil dolls! Ooooh!" He pretended to shiver.

"Cut it out," I muttered.

From where we stood, we could look down a hallway and see a door that was slightly ajar. Warm yellow light poured from the narrow crack. That was where the banging came from, too.

"What is going on in there?" Danny asked. "Let's take a look."

"Danny!" I protested. "We can't!"

He glanced at me over his shoulder. "Cluuck, Cluuck," he whispered as he tiptoed toward the door.

"Fine," I said grimly. If he could do it, so could I.

But the closer I inched to that door, the more my heart pounded.

Danny reached the door. But instead of peeking

in, he pushed the door open wider. The hinges creaked.

I swallowed. I tried to stop trembling.

Suddenly, a steely claw gripped my shoulder.

My heart dropped to my toes.

"*Don't* go in there!" a voice growled.

Chapter FOUR

I screamed and whirled around.

I stared into a hideous face, deformed by a mass of wrinkles.

The toymaker!

"Mrs. Kronck!" Danny yelped.

Mrs. Kronck? I blinked and looked again.

Yep, it was Mrs. Kronck.

Me and my stupid imagination!

"We were, uh, l-looking for you," Danny stammered.

"Right," I agreed. My heart settled back down inside my chest.

"Looking for me?" Mrs. Kronck frowned. "But I was in the kitchen. Back that way." She pointed along the hall.

"We—uh, we got lost," I said quickly.

Mrs. Kronck loosened her grip on my shoulder.

"I didn't mean to scare you," she told us. "But my husband hates to be disturbed when he's working."

She handed Danny the cup of cocoa.

"Thanks," I murmured. We hurried out of the house.

Outside, I stared at Danny. "Wow! Why is Mr. Kronck's work such a big secret? What could he be doing in there?"

Danny grinned. "I told you. He's making evil monkey dolls!"

I didn't answer. But I was thinking, maybe it's true.

Maybe he is.

I swallowed the last bite of my second piece of double chocolate chip cake.

"That was soooo good, Bess." I patted my stomach.

Danny gulped a glass of milk noisily. "Yeah. I'm stuffed," he declared.

"So will you tell us the end of the story now?" I asked.

Bess nodded as she stirred her coffee.

"The toymaker just told the little girl that the blue monkey would bring her doom," I reminded Bess.

"That's right," Bess said. "Well, at first, the little girl was very worried. But time went by, and nothing bad happened. After a while, she forgot all about what the toymaker said.

"Then one day the little girl skinned her knee at the playground. The next day, she dropped a teapot. The following Sunday, she ripped her best dress on the way to church."

"But that stuff could happen to anyone," I pointed out.

Bess raised an eyebrow. "Could it?"

"Anyway, those things aren't so bad," Danny objected. "What else happened?"

"All sorts of things." Bess shrugged. "But they weren't really awful. Just little bits of bad luck. The little girl never realized that her luck had changed. Then one day she glanced out her window and saw the family dog, Chester, chewing on the monkey in the yard. Before she could do anything, Chester started choking."

Bess stared from me to Danny. "By the time she rushed outside, Chester was dead. The monkey's arm was still in his mouth."

I shuddered. "That's awful!"

Bess nodded. "Soon after that, the little girl's father tripped over the toy monkey on the stairs and broke his leg. And then—"

I leaned forward. I didn't want to miss a word.

"—then one night," Bess continued, "the Fears' house caught fire and burned to the ground."

"Right *here*?" I gasped. In my mind, I saw a big heap of ashes where our house stood now.

Bess nodded.

"Did all the Fears die?" Danny asked.

Bess took a sip of her coffee. "The family managed to escape the fire," she said slowly. "But the next day they returned to the pile of burned wood and scattered ashes that used to be their home. And on top of one of the charred beams, the little girl saw the blue monkey. It sat there, grinning at her. It hadn't burned up. Not a single bit of its fur was even scorched."

I gasped. "Whoa!"

"The little girl grabbed the monkey and buried it next to a tree in the backyard," Bess added. "Then the family went away. No one in Shadyside has ever seen any of them again."

Buried? In the backyard?

"Wait a second!" I sat up straight in my chair. "If that story *is* true, then the monkey doll could still be buried here."

I glanced out the kitchen window.

Right in *our* backyard!

Chapter FIVE

"**D**on't open that door!" I yelled to the boy walking through the dark, gloomy house. "There's a killer behind it!"

"Amanda, chill!" Danny rolled his eyes.

It was later that night. We were watching an old episode of *The Twilight Zone*. It was one of Danny's favorite TV shows. Just hearing the theme music gave me the creeps. But I made myself watch it with Danny to prove I wasn't chicken.

I had been planning to work on a project for my art class. We were supposed to make a collage showing different parts of our lives. For weeks, I had been cutting pictures out of magazines. I was about to start pasting them to a big yellow poster board at Dad's workbench in the garage.

But after hearing Bess's spooky story about the curse of the blue monkey, I didn't want to go out to the garage by myself. What if the monkey was out there? Waiting to make something terrible happen to me?

So here I was, watching a terrifying TV show instead.

Bess went to bed half an hour before. She said Danny and I could stay up for a while on one condition—no fighting.

I nudged Danny. "You think that blue monkey doll is really buried in the backyard?" I asked him. "You think we've walked over its grave a thousand times without realizing it?"

He shrugged. "What difference does it make?" he asked. "Even if it is there, you're way too chicken to go out and dig it up."

"I am not!" I insisted.

"You are too," he insisted. "You even thought that lame story about the curse was scary. Chicken!"

I glared at him. "Stop calling me chicken!"

"*Cluuck, cluuck, cluuck!*" Danny flapped his arms at his sides as if they were chicken wings. "Let's hear it for Amanda, the Amazing Chicken Girl!"

My face grew hot. I *hated* it when Danny called me that!

"I'm *not* chicken!" I declared. I hopped off the couch. "I'm not! And I'll prove it!"

I stomped out of the den, through the kitchen, and out into the back yard. I was so mad, I wasn't even scared.

For a second, anyway.

The full moon shone brightly as I hurried toward the garden shed. I slid open the door. Half a dozen shovels hung in a row on the wall. I lifted off the biggest one. It weighed a ton.

Too heavy for me. I put it back and took a smaller shovel.

I walked out to the yard again. By now, my nerve was starting to crumble.

I tried to tell myself that it was no big deal. Lots of people probably dug up their backyards in the middle of the night. And nothing bad ever happened to them. Right?

Yeah, sure.

Then I thought of Danny making clucking noises. Flapping his arms.

I had to do this. I didn't have a choice.

I carried the shovel over to the biggest tree in our yard, a huge, ancient oak. I placed its blade against the ground and put my foot on its edge, just the way I'd seen Omar do.

"Boo!" Danny yelled from behind me.

I jumped. The shovel fell to the ground.

But I didn't let myself scream.

I gave Danny a furious look. "Shhhhh!" I hissed. I

nodded toward the house. "If Bess catches us out here in the middle of the night, you'll be in as big trouble as me."

"She won't hear a thing," Danny blustered. "She's old. She's probably hard of hearing." But I noticed he was whispering.

I turned my back on him and started digging for real. The ground was soft, thanks to my dad's constant watering. I lifted up big hunks of dirt and grass.

"Give up, Amanda," Danny whispered. "You have no idea where the monkey is buried. If there really is a blue monkey."

"Bess said it was next to a tree," I reminded him. "And there are only four trees in the backyard."

"Dad's going to ground you if he finds out you dug up his lawn looking for some stupid hundred-year-old toy," Danny said.

I shrugged. "He'll just blame it on the gophers."

The hole was about two feet deep now. And there definitely weren't any blue monkeys in it. So I stepped two paces to the right and started again.

As I pushed the shovel into the ground, the blade hit something hard.

I found it.

I found the blue monkey!

Chapter SIX

My heart thudded in my chest. "Hey, I found it!" I whispered to Danny.

I heaved up a chunk of Dad's precious lawn—and saw a big rock.

"Oh, yeah, that really looks like a toy monkey," Danny scoffed. "Nice going, Amanda!"

I did my best to ignore him and kept digging.

By the time I started my sixth hole, I was sweating. "This is harder than I thought," I admitted. "You know, if you dug too, it would go faster."

"Not a chance." Danny shook his head. "I bet Bess made up the whole story about the blue monkey anyway." He rubbed his hands up and down over his arms. "It's getting cold out here. Come on. Let's go inside. I want to work on my model plane."

I gazed down at my hands. I was starting to get a blister on one palm. The muscles in my back ached.

I sighed. "Okay. I'll try the other trees tomorrow night."

I hung up the shovel in the shed. Tomorrow I would ask Bess for a few more details about where the blue monkey was buried.

I believed in the monkey. All that stuff about how the blue monkey made the little girl's dog choke, and made her dad fall and break his leg . . . Bess couldn't have made all of that up.

Could she?

When I came out of the shed, clouds were blowing across the moon. I couldn't see a thing as I made my way across the lawn.

"Danny?" I called. "Where are you?"

No answer.

"Danny?"

Still nothing.

If Danny was planning to sneak up on me again, Chicken Amanda was going to let him have it!

Then my brother's terrified scream echoed through the night.

"Aaaaaaaaaaaaaaaaaaaaaaaaaaagh!"

I froze. "Danny?" I cried. "Where are you?"

My voice shook with fear.

The blue monkey! Had it gotten Danny?

"I—I'm over here," Danny called.

I let out a sigh. At least he was alive!

I peered in the direction of his voice. It came from the base of a big maple. But all I could see was a dark shape on the ground.

I ran over to the shape. It was Danny. He was sitting on the ground, holding his leg.

"What happened?" I demanded.

"My foot got caught in one of the stupid gopher holes," he moaned.

"Can you get up?" I asked.

Danny shook his head. "It's stuck," he said. "Really stuck."

I crouched down next to Danny. "Wow, this is some gopher hole," I remarked. His leg had disappeared into the ground almost up to his knee.

"Wiggle your foot around," I suggested. "Maybe it'll loosen up."

Danny shook his head again. "I think it's caught in some tree roots or something. It won't budge."

"I'll get a shovel," I decided. I jumped up. "Don't move."

"Ha ha," Danny called after me as I ran to the shed.

I came back and started digging away the ground around Danny's leg. Luckily, the moon came out from behind the clouds, so I could see what I was doing.

"Try now," I ordered, offering him a hand.

Danny gripped my outstretched hand and I

heaved. His foot slid out of the deep hole. He hopped a few times, gaining his balance, and caught himself against the tree.

"Whoa," he groaned, rubbing his ankle. "Lucky for you I didn't break my leg. It would have been all your fault."

I rolled my eyes. "You're welcome."

Danny began limping toward the house. I bent down for one last look at the hole.

And then I saw it.

A squared-off shape. One corner glinted in the moonlight.

It definitely wasn't a rock.

"Hey! What's this?" I grabbed the shovel and poked around in the hole. "Something's down there, Danny."

"Dig it up," Danny ordered.

I was too excited to think about the blister on my hand. I dug like crazy.

At last the rectangular thing was uncovered. I knelt down. With both hands, I reached into the hole and pulled out a metal box. It was about the size of a shoe box.

I glanced up at Danny.

His eyes met mine.

I could tell he was wondering the same thing I was.

What was in the box?

Chapter SEVEN

"**L**et me see." Danny grabbed the box from me.

My heart was racing. I wanted him to rip off the lid. But at the same time, I was afraid.

Danny brushed off some dirt and read the faint letters on the old tin box: "Onida's Crispy Crackers." He handed me the box. "Here, Amanda. Have a cracker."

I giggled nervously and held the box up.

"Open it!" Danny urged.

"You think it's the monkey?" I asked. My heart pounded.

"We'll never know if you don't open it," Danny snapped.

I shook the box gently.

Something clanked inside.

It definitely wasn't crackers.

I ran a finger over the lid. "Let's open it in the morning," I suggested. Nothing was as scary in the bright light of day.

Danny snorted. He grabbed the box out of my hands and yanked off the lid. "Tah-dah!"

I gasped.

The blue monkey lay in the box.

Its face, hands, and feet were carved out of wood. The rest of its body was covered with thick blue fur.

The monkey stared up with one coal-black eye. The other eye was missing. It lay unmoving in the box—as if in a coffin.

It seemed to be glaring at me.

A chill ran down my back. I glanced from the monkey doll to Danny.

"So Bess's story *is* true," I whispered.

"Then I guess you're cursed!" Danny said gleefully. "Just like the little girl in the story!"

"Well, if I'm cursed, so are you!" I cried.

"No way." Danny shook his head. "You dug up the box—not me. The monkey is yours. You're doomed!"

"You opened the lid," I reminded him. "You saw the monkey first."

Danny ignored me. "Cursed, cursed, cursed," he chanted. "Amanda is cursed!"

I was getting very tired of him. Besides, my muscles ached from digging and my blister hurt. "I'm going in," I told Danny. "Here." I held out the blue monkey to him.

He dodged away.

Hah!

"What's the matter?" I sneered. "Scared?"

"Who, me? Get real." Danny grabbed the monkey by one ear and whisked it out of the box. "I'm taking it inside so we can ask Bess about it tomorrow." And he started for the house.

"Why ask about it if you don't believe in curses anyway?" I challenged.

Danny grinned at me. "Hey—what do I know?"

We took off our muddy shoes and left them on the back porch. Then we went inside.

As we walked through the dark den, Danny tossed the blue monkey on the couch. He ran up the stairs.

I followed. As I started up the stairs, I glanced back at the monkey.

I gasped.

Its one black eye was glowing an evil orange in the dark.

A second later I realized that the orange glow was just a reflection from the hall light. "Whew," I muttered.

It's not evil, I told myself. It's just a toy.

Right?

I couldn't breathe. I tried to scream for help. But

my voice choked inside my throat. A rope was tightening around my neck.

Someone was trying to strangle me!

My eyes popped open. I was in my bed. It was pitch dark. I grabbed at the rope around my throat. Was I dreaming?

No! This was real! The rope was tightening—cutting off my air. I couldn't breathe!

I twisted and turned, gasping for breath. I yanked at the rope. It squeezed tighter.

If I couldn't get it off, I was finished!

I made a last desperate pull at the rope.

Suddenly I was free. I sucked in a huge gulp of air.

I sat up and stared wildly around.

Who was trying to kill me?

Moonlight streamed in through my bedroom window. Beside my pillow was my top sheet. One end of it was twisted tightly together. Like a rope.

I let out a sigh of relief. No one was trying to strangle me. I must have been having a wild dream. I got tangled up in my sheet. That's all.

Trying to calm down, I climbed out of bed and walked over to my window. It overlooked the back yard.

The sky showed streaks of pink now. Almost dawn.

Everything looked so peaceful. So safe.

My breathing began to return to normal. I was

about to turn from the window when a movement caught my eye.

Someone was in our yard!

The back of my neck prickled with fear. I squinted, trying to see through the thick shadows.

The someone had on dark clothing and a baseball cap.

Omar! It was only Omar!

I sighed with relief. The guy worked pretty strange hours. Here he was at dawn, standing over a gopher hole. Did he ever sleep?

As if he heard my thoughts, Omar suddenly turned and stared directly at my window. His one eye seemed to burn into my gaze. He bared his teeth in a horrible, silent growl.

Yikes! I jumped away from the window. I dove for my bed.

But as I landed on it, I froze.

All I could do was stare in disbelief.

On my pillow sat the blue monkey, staring at me with one gleaming black eye.

I clapped a hand over my mouth to stifle a scream.

What was the monkey doing in my bed?

Danny left it on the couch.

In my mind, I pictured the monkey scuttling up the stairs. Creeping into my room. Climbing onto my bed.

I shuddered. I grabbed the thing off my pillow and hurled it to the floor. I didn't want it near me!

Okay, Amanda, calm down, I told myself. Take it easy.

I knew what I needed—a nice, hot shower. It would clear my head—and wash off some of last night's dirt. Besides, it was practically time to get up.

I grabbed my blue terrycloth robe from a hook in my closet and headed for the bathroom. I couldn't wait to feel the warm, soothing water splashing down on me.

I pushed open the door and walked into the bathroom.

"Ew!" I cried as my foot slid on something wet and sticky.

I stepped back to see what it was.

My eyes widened in horror.

A spreading stain covered the white tile floor.

A *red* stain.

It was blood.

Bright red blood!

Chapter EIGHT

I screamed. And kept on screaming.

Blood was everywhere.

The white tiled floor was covered with it.

I was standing in a puddle of blood!

I couldn't seem to move. And I couldn't stop screaming.

Not when Danny ran into the bathroom.

Not when Bess ran in right behind him, tying the sash of her bathrobe.

I didn't stop screaming until Bess put her hands on my shoulders and shook me. "Take a deep breath, Amanda," she urged.

"And if your nose is working, you'll stop freaking," Danny added.

My nose? What was he talking about?

I took a breath. I smelled something familiar . . . Strawberries.

I smelled strawberries!

My eyes traveled across the bathroom. Next to the tub, I spotted my new, giant economy-sized bottle of strawberry shampoo. It was lying on its side. The cap was off. And the bright red shampoo had run out all over the floor.

Oh.

"Sorry I screamed," I murmured. I felt like an idiot.

"That's okay," Bess said soothingly.

"I thought it was . . . blood," I tried to explain.

"Oh, that's an easy mistake to make," Danny scoffed. He sat on the edge of the tub to rinse the shampoo off his feet.

"I—I had a bad night," I stammered.

"I'm going back to bed," Danny announced, and stomped off.

"Well, I'm not. I'm awake now. I'll help you clean this mess up, Amanda," Bess offered.

"No, that's okay," I said quickly. "I'll mop it up with an old towel. It's no big deal."

Bess gave me a wink. "That's right. It's just a bit of bad luck," she told me. "That's all."

When they were gone, I cleaned up the gooey shampoo. Then I jumped into the shower. The warm water felt good.

By the time I was done I felt much better. I stepped out of the shower and dried myself. I was lucky to get two sudsings out of the strawberry shampoo left in the bottle, I thought.

Then my hand stopped moving.

Lucky.

What did Bess say about luck? That spilling the shampoo was a bit of bad luck?

The good feeling left me. In Bess's story, nothing too terrible happened to the little girl at first. Nothing she noticed. Just little bits of bad luck.

Was my luck changing too?

Was the spilled shampoo the beginning of the curse?

No! It couldn't be!

But what about the sheet tying itself around my neck?

Was that part of the curse, too?

No. That was silly. It could happen to anyone. Any time.

I bent down to dry my toes.

When I straightened up, I was face to face with the blue monkey!

The monkey's horrible face seemed to be smiling at me. I clapped a hand over my mouth to keep from screaming again.

Then I stepped back—and saw that the monkey wasn't really there.

I was staring at its reflection in the bathroom mirror!

It was still in my room, where I left it.

But—wait a minute.

I turned away from the mirror and gazed into my bedroom.

I remembered throwing the monkey on the floor. But it wasn't on the floor any more.

The blue monkey was sitting on my pillow again!

Anger rose inside me. I was furious! I wasn't going to let that stupid monkey make me feel cursed!

I threw on my robe and stormed out of the bathroom into my bedroom. My hand shook as I reached for the toy.

I grabbed that furry blue menace and stuffed him into the trash can in the hall.

"There!" I exclaimed. "Now you're nothing but trash!"

I wadded up some paper and stuffed it on top of the monkey. I kept going until I couldn't see one bit of blue fur.

I let out a breath. Now I could forget about the monkey. Tomorrow was garbage pick-up day. The garbage men would take the horrible thing to the dump. Then I would be rid of it forever!

As I stood there, I glanced out the hall window.

A light was on in the Kroncks' house. I could see right into a room.

I squinted. It wasn't a room I recognized from last night.

Mr. Kronck suddenly wheeled into view. It hit me then—this was the room we tried to peek into. The workshop!

Mr. Kronck wheeled close to the window. Why was he up so early? I wondered. Or—did he work all night?

He held something in his lap—a book. A very big one.

Then I saw something in his hand. I gasped.

It was a long, sharp knife!

Mr. Kronck sliced the air with it. He waved his other hand crazily around.

I stood frozen at the window. What was he doing? Mrs. Kronck's words came back into my head: *You don't want to know.*

I stared. Mr. Kronck wheeled around the room, stabbing the knife at the air over and over. Every now and then he stopped and studied the book in his lap. Then he would start stabbing again.

Was the old man performing some sort of evil magic ritual?

Or was he practicing murdering someone with a long, sharp knife?

I stepped back from the window, chilled.

There was something very, very wrong with Mr. Kronck.

What if he was the toymaker from Bess's story?

"He couldn't be," I muttered as I went into my room to dress. The toymaker was already a grown-up fifty years ago. He must be dead by now!

Unless he used magic to keep himself alive, a little voice suggested. He was supposed to be a sorcerer, after all.

"Forget it!" I ordered myself. My stupid imagination was running away with me again. That was all.

Anyway, the curse of the blue monkey couldn't get me. I did what the little girl in the story should have done fifty years earlier. I threw that horrible toy away!

I ran downstairs and ate a fast breakfast. Then I headed to the garage to work on my collage.

Last night, I was afraid to go into the garage alone. But not now. "There's nothing to be afraid of," I reminded myself. I hurried through the door from the kitchen to the garage.

Then I stopped in horror.

My dad's workbench was a total mess. All the pictures I had cut out for my collage were wadded up or torn to bits. And my sheet of yellow poster board was ripped down the middle.

The curse!

Fear spread through me. Already this morning I had almost been strangled by my sheet. I had waded into shampoo that I thought was blood. Now my proejct was ruined!

I glanced at my watch. It was only ten after eight.

What else might happen by lunchtime? I didn't even want to think about it!

I walked over to the workbench, trying to figure out where to start cleaning up. I reached for the poster board.

My hand froze in midair.

There on a shelf above the workbench sat the blue monkey.

Its hideous face seemed to mock me. Its one eye seemed to glow like a hot coal.

My stomach churned.

I was cursed! Doomed!

Then I heard a shuffling noise behind me.

I spun around—and gasped.

What I saw was much, much worse than the blue monkey.

Chapter NINE

"**D**anny!" I cried.

My brother stood behind me, laughing his head off.

The minute I saw him, I knew what was going on.

"Gotcha!" he cried. "Boy, did I ever scare you, Chicken Amanda!" He laughed even harder.

I crossed my arms over my chest and glared at him.

He kept laughing. "*I* spilled your stinky shampoo last night! *I* put the monkey on your bed while you were in the shower!" he exclaimed. "It was all me!"

My hands clenched into fists. "You are the biggest jerk in the universe!" I cried. "How could you do that to me? How could you wreck my art project?"

"You call a few pictures cut out of a magazine an

art project?" Danny rolled his eyes. "I wish you could have seen your face when you spotted that monkey! You went *bananas*!"

I was so mad I couldn't even think of what to say. Even for Danny, this was a horrible, mean, trick. I couldn't believe my brother would go so far.

That was when a terrifying idea hit me.

What if something was *making* Danny act even meaner than usual?

What if . . .

I marched over to the workbench and snatched the monkey off the shelf. I held it out at arm's length. I didn't want it close to me. I stormed into the kitchen with it, yelling, "Bess! Bess! Where are you, Bess?"

Danny ran in behind me.

Bess sat at the kitchen table in her bathrobe drinking a cup of coffee. "I'm right here," she pointed out in a calm voice.

"Look!" I held up the monkey. "We dug it up last night."

Bess didn't appear all that surprised. She set her coffee cup down on the table and took the furry toy from my hand. She turned it over, examining it closely.

"So," she said at last, "you found the monkey." She set the toy down on the table. Its one beady eye stared at nothing.

I nodded. "See, Danny tripped in a gopher hole and when I dug him out, I saw—"

"Bess doesn't want to hear every detail," Danny cut in.

"Danny brought the monkey into the house last night," I went on. "I think it's putting a curse on us. See, Danny's been playing tricks on me with the monkey—putting it on my bed and things—" I shot Danny a look. I hoped he appreciated the fact that I wasn't tattling on him for the bloody shampoo mess. Or for destroying my art project.

"Danny!" Bess exclaimed. "You shouldn't play tricks on your sister. That isn't nice."

"Oh, can't she take a joke?" Danny muttered.

"What I'm trying to say," I went on, "is that I think the monkey's curse is *making* Danny do these awful things. It's making him bring me bad luck."

Bess smiled. "That's silly. There's no curse on this monkey, Amanda."

I frowned. "But you said—"

Bess picked up the monkey again. "Besides, according to the story, the monkey's curse doesn't start until someone *gives* it to you. The person must say, 'It's a gift.'" Bess handed me the monkey. "Otherwise," she added, "there is no curse."

Frowning, I set the monkey back down on the table. I had to admit the thing looked pretty harmless. Lying there with sunlight streaming in through the

46

kitchen windows, it seemed like any old stuffed toy.

I started to feel dumb.

"Chicken Amanda!" Danny yelled for the hundredth time. "She's afraid of a stuffed monkey!"

"Danny!" Bess scolded. "Stop teasing Amanda."

Danny's laughing face made me furious. My brother had gone over the top. He needed to be taught a lesson.

I'll get you back, I silently vowed. And when I do, you'll never pull one of your stupid tricks on me again!

It rained that day. I spent most of it up in my room, cutting out more magazine pictures for my art project.

Bess cooked us spaghetti with tomato sauce for supper. It was tasty, but dinner wasn't much fun. Every time I glanced over at him, Danny pumped his arms up and down as if they were wings, doing his Chicken Amanda imitation.

I was tired of Danny. I was tired, period. I hadn't gotten much sleep the night before.

Bess turned in about ten o'clock, and so did I. I changed, then went into the bathroom to brush my teeth.

I was rinsing my mouth out when I felt the hairs on the back of my neck stand up.

A horrible yell ripped through the house.

Chapter TEN

The yell came from Danny's room!

My bathrobe flapped around me as I raced down the hall. I was reaching for his doorknob when the door swung open.

"My plane is missing!" he shouted. "My model Spitfire! It was right here before dinner. And now look!"

Danny aimed a finger at the small wooden table he used for making models. Except for a small tube of glue and a few spare parts, the surface was bare.

"I've been working on it all summer!" he cried. "I put the last piece on it today! I can't believe this!"

I shook my head. "That's awful," I said sympathetically. "Do you think the monkey stole it?"

"No, I don't think the stupid monkey stole it. I don't know what happened to it, but it's gone!" Danny kicked at the table. "Ow!" He hopped up and down on one leg. "That hurt!"

"Bad luck, Danny," I murmured. Then a grin broke across my face. I couldn't help it. "I guess you don't like it when something of *yours* disappears—any more than I like having something of mine ruined."

"Huh?" Danny stopped hopping. "*You* took my plane?"

"What's the matter?" I taunted. "Can't you take a joke?"

Danny glared at me. "I want it back *now*, Amanda."

"Only if you promise to quit calling me chicken," I shot back.

He looked ready to explode. "Fine. I promise," he muttered. "The plane, Amanda. Now!"

"Follow me." I led the way down the hall. "I hid it while you were downstairs watching *Invasion of the Spider People*."

I opened the door of the linen closet. "Here it is."

Danny pushed past me.

"Amanda!" he shrieked. "What have you done?"

"What?" I stared at him.

"You wrecked it!" he yelled. "I can't believe you did that!"

I had put the plane on top of a red towel. I was

really careful with it. Now I gazed at the towel and gasped.

It was a smashed mess of plane parts. It looked as if someone had sat on it!

"I didn't break it, Danny!" I protested. "I swear."

Danny didn't say anything. He just stared at what was left of his model plane.

"I'm really sorry, Danny," I went on. "I didn't mean for this to happen. I don't know how it could have—"

I stopped talking.

I noticed something sticking out from under the red towel.

Something blue and furry.

"Danny," I whispered. "The monkey!"

The light in the hallway was dim. But I could see Danny's face turn pale. He lifted the red towel.

The monkey lay under it.

Danny stepped back. "Its eye—" he whispered. "It's really glowing!"

I nodded. I felt very cold all of a sudden.

I knew that Danny didn't know the plane was in the closet, so he never would have put the monkey there. Danny would never have smashed his model plane for a joke. I hadn't put the monkey in the closet, much less hidden it under a towel.

So how did it get there?

I could only think of one explanation.

Bess was wrong. There really was a curse on the monkey.

And we were its newest victims.

I grabbed the monkey and pulled it out of the closet. The glow in its eye was gone again.

"Let's go into your room," Danny suggested in a low voice. "We need to talk."

I nodded. I wasn't mad at Danny anymore. I was just scared. And I knew he was, too.

In my room, I perched the blue monkey on the corner of my dresser. I decided the best thing to do was to keep it in plain view—where I could keep an eye on it.

I plopped onto my bed. Danny sat on my desk chair.

"You're telling the truth, right, Amanda?" he asked. "You didn't break my airplane and do all this monkey stuff just to cover it up?"

"No way." I put my hand over my heart. "I didn't break your plane. And I didn't go anywhere *near* the monkey after we were talking to Bess in the kitchen."

"I believe you," Danny said. "You're not a good enough liar to pull something like this over on me."

I let the insult slide. I didn't want to waste time arguing. We needed to figure out what to do about the monkey curse—before it was too late.

"This is beyond freaky," I murmured. "I feel like

we're in some episode of *Unsolved Phenomena.*"

"There must be a reasonable explanation." Danny stared at the ceiling. "Hey! Maybe Bess hid the monkey in the closet so we'd quit fighting about it."

I considered the idea. "Nah," I decided. "She wouldn't smash up your plane."

"True." Danny paused, frowning. "I hate to say this . . ."

"You hate to say what?" I asked. But I knew the answer.

"Maybe the monkey really is cursed," he whispered. "I mean, I guess *anything* is possible."

"It seems like the only explanation," I agreed. "But—"

SLAM!

I whipped my head around toward the noise.

The door to my bedroom had banged shut. And the toy monkey was sitting on the floor, in front of the door. Its one eye glowed even brighter than before.

"How did it do that?" Danny whispered. His voice shook.

"I don't know. Let's get out of here!" I cried.

I leaped off the bed. Danny was right behind me. We rushed to the door—stepping around the monkey.

I grabbed the knob and pulled—hard.

Nothing happened.

"Let me," Danny exclaimed. He shoved my hand aside and gripped the knob. He twisted until his knuckles turned white.

But the door stayed closed.

The curse had sealed it shut!

Chapter ELEVEN

"**B**ess!" I cried. "Bess, help us!"

She won't hear," Danny grunted as he tugged at the door. "She sleeps through everything."

He yanked on the knob once more. Then he let go.

"It's totally stuck!" he panted.

We were trapped. Trapped with the blue monkey!

I hated that stupid monkey! I drew back my leg and kicked it across the room.

Danny and I moved away from the door. My eyes searched the room for something—anything—we could use to get the door open.

"There's my baseball bat," I told Danny, pointing. "By my dresser. Maybe we could use the bat to break down the door."

Danny ran to the bat. But as he reached for it, something flew through the air toward him.

"Look out!" I shrieked.

He ducked. The thing smashed into the wall right behind his head. It shattered into a thousand pieces.

For a second, I was too stunned to move. Then I ran over to Danny. "Are you okay?" I asked him.

"Yeah." Danny nodded. "What was that thing?"

I bent down to examine the pieces of—what?—on the floor. I picked up a shard. "It looks like pink china," I said. "No, wait—it's the conch shell from my shell collection!"

I ran to my window. Danny followed with the bat in his hand.

The rest of my shells were still on the sill. But there was a space where the conch had been.

"That thing flew across the room!" Danny exclaimed. "It almost killed me. It—"

Danny broke off and stared out the window.

I did, too.

Mr. Kronck was wheeling around his workshop again.

"He's laughing his head off," Danny murmured.

I saw that Mr. Kronck still had the book on his lap.

"What's he holding in his left hand?" I asked. It looked like a long piece of dark cloth.

"I can't see," Danny said.

As if he heard us, Mr. Kronck suddenly held up the thing in his hand. We could both see it now. He shook it madly in the air, laughing like crazy.

"It's a doll!" Danny cried.

I gasped. Danny was right. It was a doll.

A horrible, headless doll!

Danny and I stared at each other in horror.

Mr. Kronck really *was* making evil dolls in his workshop!

Now we knew.

Mr. Kronck was the evil toymaker!

"We have to get out of—*noooo!*" I screamed.

The pencil jar flew off my desk. The entire jar headed right for me!

I screamed and covered my head with my arms.

The jar struck the window frame with a mighty crash. Pens and pencils sprayed all over the room.

"Come on!" Danny grabbed my hand.

He yanked me across the room. He grabbed the doorknob again. This time, it turned easily in his hand.

I glanced back over my shoulder.

"The monkey!" I shouted. "Look!"

The monkey wasn't sprawled on the floor where I'd kicked it.

It was sitting on my bed.

"Wait!" I called to Danny.

I wrenched my hand from his grip. I ran back into my room and grabbed the monkey.

"We're getting rid of this thing *right now*!" I told Danny.

"I know how we can get rid of it for good," Danny whispered as we raced down the stairs. "We'll barbecue it on the grill!"

"Yes!" I exclaimed. "We'll burn it until there's nothing left but a pile of ashes!" For once, my brother and I were in complete agreement.

"But—wait a second." I stopped at the foot of the stairs. "When the Fears' house burned down, the monkey didn't burn."

"Who knows if it was even in the house?" Danny argued. "We're going to put it on the grill and stand there and *watch* it burn. Come on!"

For the second night in a row, Danny and I were sneaking around way past our bedtimes. Lucky for us Bess was such a heavy sleeper!

We hurried through the kitchen. I grabbed a pack of matches from a jar on the counter. Then we went to the garage.

Danny rolled the grill out to the driveway and went back for a bag of charcoal. He emptied it into the grill and began spreading it out evenly with a poker.

"Hurry!" I urged. I didn't want to spend one more minute with the horrible blue monkey!

I shivered. The night was cold. The moon, which had shone brightly last night, was now covered by thick, stormy clouds. Somewhere down the block, a cat yowled.

Danny poured on some lighter fluid, then positioned the wire rack on the grill.

"Ve are ready for zee meat!" he said, trying to sound like a French chef.

I placed the blue monkey on top of the rack and handed Danny the matches.

"Good-bye, curse!" Danny called.

He struck a match and tossed it onto the charcoal. The briquettes burst into flame.

Danny and I stood there, watching and waiting.

Suddenly the blaze shot up higher. The fire crackled—and the blue monkey was swallowed up in flames.

"All right!" Danny pumped his fist in the air triumphantly.

"Finally!" I added. Relief washed over me. "That's the end of the blue monkey."

A bright orange torch of flame suddenly leapt six feet in the air. Another flame joined it. And another.

Danny and I watched, open-mouthed, and the flames jumped up into the cold night air.

Then the grill began to spit little bursts of fire.

Right at us!

A fat spark hit my arm. I felt its searing heat.

"Ow!" I cried. "Danny!"

But the fire was spitting out giant sparks at Danny too!

He jumped up and down, wildly trying to brush them off his clothes. Out of his hair.

Then a fireball the size of a baseball whizzed by my head.

In a second, fireballs were zooming at us, thick and fast.

Danny and I were about to burn!

Chapter TWELVE

"**R**un!" I cried.

Danny and I slapped at the crackling fireballs as we ran. They glowed orange against the night sky. *HSSS! ZZZZZT!* They shot past our heads.

By the time we made it to the end of the driveway, the fireballs were falling short of us. At last the flames settled back into the grill.

We stood on the sidewalk, gasping for breath. I brushed at the scorched spots on my robe, making sure they weren't still smoldering. An awful burnt smell hung in the air.

"The flames attacked us!" Danny exclaimed.

I nodded. "Maybe that's how curses end," I said hopefully. "With a bang."

But somehow I doubted it.

From the end of the driveway, we watched the fiery grill. The flames began to burn down. Soon they were hardly more than a red glow.

"Let's go see what happened to the monkey," Danny whispered.

I grabbed his arm as we started back up the drive. If he called me chicken, I was going to pop him one.

Luckily for him, he didn't.

We peered down at the wire rack on the grill.

There was nothing on it.

Nothing at all. Not even a pile of ashes.

"The monkey's gone," Danny whispered. "It must have burned up completely."

I shivered. "Then why don't I feel safe now?"

Danny turned and gazed across the street.

"Because of Kronck," he said. "Because he's the evil toymaker. He can put another curse on us any time he wants."

"But why would he?" I asked.

"Don't ask me," Danny snapped. "I don't know how evil toymakers think."

"You know what *I* think?" I said slowly. "I think we have to do more than destroy the monkey." Did you see the big book on Mr. Kronck's lap? It must be a book of magic spells. Maybe if we destroy it, we'll be safe."

"Okay," Danny agreed. "Let's go over there."

"What, *now*?" I cried. "Are you crazy? I was thinking tomorrow. I was thinking in the daytime."

"We'll just look around tonight," Danny argued. "Come on. Don't be a chicken."

I sighed. Then I tightened the sash of my bathrobe around my waist.

"Okay," I mumbled. "Lead the way."

We crossed the street and started up the Kroncks' walk. My heart was pounding in my ears like a drum.

I glanced at the picture window on the right. That was where we saw Mr. Kronck holding up the headless doll earlier.

Dark drapes covered the window now. No light shone out from behind them.

"I don't think Mr. Kronck is in his workshop," I whispered.

Danny nodded to show he'd heard me. Then he stood on tiptoe to peer into the little glass window at the top of the door.

As he pressed forward against it, the door swung open.

I caught my breath. But there was no one behind the door. It must simply have been unlocked.

Danny glanced over his shoulder at me. Then he stepped silently into the creepy old house.

Every inch of me quaked with fear.

What if this was Mr. Kronck's night to do his knife tricks?

But I couldn't let Danny go in there alone.

I took a deep breath and followed him inside.

The house seemed spookier than ever on this dark night. It was totally still. The dusty air seemed to choke me. I could hardly breathe. But somehow my feet kept moving after Danny.

We crept closer and closer to the workshop. With every step, I felt more terrified.

Danny reached the door. We paused for a moment.

Then, very slowly, Danny turned the knob.

He pushed the door open a crack. We peered in.

I was wrong about Mr. Kronck not being in the workshop.

He was there, wheeling around in his chair.

The book of spells sat on his lap. But I barely noticed it.

I was staring in horror at what was in his hand.

The knife!

Mr. Kronck slashed the air with the long, gleaming blade. Over and over he stabbed at an invisible victim. As he slashed, he muttered, "Die! Die, and I'll dance on your grave!"

I bit my tongue to keep from screaming. Danny and I took one look at each other.

Then we turned and ran for the door.

Together we burst out into the cold night air. We ran down the Kroncks' walk.

We had just crossed the street when a loud voice boomed out behind us.

"Hey, you kids! Stop! Stop right where you are!"

Chapter THIRTEEN

Caught!

The voice was so commanding. I couldn't help myself. I skidded to a stop.

So did Danny. This time, *he* grabbed *my* arm.

We huddled together, trembling. Waiting for evil Mr. Kronck to come wheeling down upon us.

But he didn't.

Instead, I saw a tall figure striding toward us. A figure with wild white hair. And a patch over one eye.

"Omar!" I gasped.

My heart slowed down.

Danny let go of my arm.

"Boy, are we glad to see *you*, Omar!" I exclaimed.

Omar loomed over us, frowning.

"What are you kids doing, running around at this time of night?" he growled.

"We—uh, it's sort of a long story," I mumbled.

"What are *you* doing here in the middle of the night?" Danny shot back.

Omar's single line of bushy white eyebrows arched up. "Gophers are rodents," he rumbled. "Nocturnal. Night's the best time to catch them."

Boy, was this guy ever obsessed with gophers!

"Why did you yell at us to stop?" I asked him.

"Didn't want you running around your yard in the dark," Omar said. "Dangerous. You could break your ankle tripping in one of those gopher holes."

"Tell me about it," Danny muttered.

"Stay out of the backyard, kids," Omar warned in a low voice. Then he tipped his old, worn-out baseball cap and drifted away down Fear Street.

Danny and I walked up our driveway. My heartbeat was almost back to normal by now.

"Omar's a creep," Danny complained as he rolled the charcoal grill back into the garage.

"Yeah," I agreed. "But at least he isn't an evil toymaker."

We went into the kitchen. I spotted what was left of Bess's chocolate chip cake on the counter. Suddenly I was starving.

"I'm going to have a piece of cake before I go to bed," I told Danny. "Want me to cut you one?"

"Sure." Danny nodded. "Anyway, we should celebrate—the blue monkey is burned to a crisp!"

I took two plates out of the cabinet. Then I removed the glass cover from the cake.

"I wish Bess had never told us that story," Danny admitted.

"Me, too," I agreed. I reached for a long knife that hung on the knife rack.

CLANK! It fell to the counter. Pain shot through my hand.

"Ow!" I yelled.

I glanced down.

Blood was all over the counter.

Not bright red strawberry shampoo, but dark red blood.

My blood!

The knife had sliced right through my palm!

"Owwww!" I cried. My whole hand throbbed with pain.

"Whoa, Amanda!" Danny shouted.

I clutched my injured hand and sank into one of the kitchen chairs.

Danny grabbed a dish towel and wrapped it around my hand to stop the bleeding. "What happened?"

"I—I was about to cut the cake," I told him. "I don't know what happened. All of a sudden, there was . . . all this blood."

Danny sat down by me. He peeled away the dish towel and peered at the wound.

"Looks pretty bad," he muttered. "I'll help you

wash it and put some antiseptic on it."

Danny led me over to the sink. I tried not to look at all the blood.

"Do—do you think I'll need stitches?" I asked anxiously.

Danny only shrugged as he turned on the cold water to a gentle stream.

"Stick your hand under here," he ordered. "That way we can see how deep the cut is."

I closed my eyes and thrust my hand under the cold water.

When I opened my eyes, most of the blood had washed down the drain. My skin looked very white.

"It's not too deep," Danny said. He pulled out the box of bandages Mom keeps for kitchen emergencies. "You'll be okay."

"I wish Mom and Dad were here," I moaned as Danny stretched three bandages across the cut.

Suddenly Danny's eyes widened.

"Amanda," he breathed.

He was staring in the direction of the refrigerator. His face was pale, and his hands started shaking.

"What?" I turned to see what he was looking at.

I gasped.

On top of the refrigerator sat the blue monkey!

Its eye glowed like fire.

"No!" I cried. "It can't be!"

"It is," Danny whispered. "It's back!"

Chapter Fourteen

"**H**ow can the monkey be sitting up there?" I yelped. "We burned it up! We checked the grill—it was totally gone!"

Danny swallowed. "I guess it wasn't," he whispered.

"Then we *are* doomed!" I cried. "If fire couldn't get rid of the monkey and its evil curse—what can?"

Suddenly I felt exhausted. "Let's talk to Bess," I said.

I needed a grown-up. Someone who would tell me not to worry. That there was no curse on the blue monkey.

Danny nodded. "Hope she doesn't mind getting up at—," he checked his watch: "—two-thirty in the morning."

"Two-thirty!" I repeated. "Wow!"

Danny and I climbed the stairs. Bess was staying in Mom and Dad's bedroom, at the far end of the hall from our bedrooms.

I knocked softly on the door. "Bess?" I murmured.

There was no answer.

I knocked again. Still nothing.

"Bess!" I called in a louder voice.

Silence.

Danny opened the door. "Bess?" he called.

The lamp was on. But the bed was still made up.

The room was empty.

I turned to Danny. He looked as confused as I felt.

"Weird," he muttered. "Where would she go at this time of night?"

My heart started thumping again. Why would Bess leave us all alone in the middle of the night? Where could she be?

Did something happen to her?

We ran back downstairs.

"Bess!" Danny yelled. Where are you?"

No answer.

The living room was empty. So was the den. We walked back into the kitchen. The monkey still sat on the refrigerator.

"Look." Danny nodded toward the door to the basement. It was slightly ajar. "Was that open before?"

"I don't think so," I replied, frowning. I walked

over to the door and opened it wider. It was dark down there.

"Bess?" I called.

She didn't answer. I knew she wouldn't. After all, who hangs out in a pitch-dark basement in the middle of the night?

"What if something terrible happened to her?" I whispered.

"We have to go back to the Kroncks'," Danny stated.

"What? Why?" I cried. "So Mr. Kronck can stab us?"

Danny didn't crack a smile. "Amanda, it's getting worse. The way you cut yourself—that could have been really bad. And now Bess has vanished. This whole curse thing is getting too dangerous. We have to stop Mr. Kronck!"

I swallowed hard and nodded. Danny was right. We had to find a way to break the curse—or we were going to die!

"I'm going across the street," Danny declared. "If you want to stay here alone with the blue monkey, that's your business."

When he put it that way, the choice became pretty clear.

"Let's go," I agreed. "And let's hope Mr. Kronck is in bed!"

So we headed for the toymaker's creaky old house—again.

The sky was as dark as ever. I smelled rain in the air.

When we reached the Kroncks', Danny pushed the door open and we slipped inside.

"I'm not sure this is such a good idea," I whispered as we tiptoed toward the workshop.

Was Mr. Kronck in there?

Would he be waiting for us, clutching his knife?

The workshop door wasn't closed all the way.

Somewhere inside the room, a light was burning.

I shivered with fear as I followed Danny down the ramp that led to the workshop. My gaze darted around the dimly-lit room.

Then I let out a sigh of relief.

Mr. Kronck wasn't there.

A small lamp shone on a cluttered desk in the corner of the room. Large bookcases lined the walls. In the middle of the room stood a large wooden work table.

It didn't exactly look like the workshop of a mad toy-maker. There were no wood-working tools. No blocks about to be carved into dolls—or blue monkeys.

Then I saw how wrong I was.

I clutched Danny's arm.

"Look! Over there!" I whispered hoarsely.

Sitting on top of the desk was the body of the horrible headless doll!

"It's just a doll," Danny told me. "Chill, Amanda.

Try to keep your mind on why we're here. We have to find a way to break the curse!"

I nodded, trying to make myself calm down.

Together, we walked over to the desk. Beside the lamp was an ancient typewriter. It was so old, it didn't even plug in.

Danny picked up a sheet from a stack of papers lying next to it. "Listen to this!" he whispered. He started reading. "'The toy strangles the little girl. She screams, but she's helpless. Within seconds, she can't breathe.'"

I felt the blood draining from my face. Strangled?

Was that a description of what happened to *me* the night before?

Did Mr. Kronck really make the toy monkey strangle me with my sheet?

"Go on," I urged Danny. "Keep reading!"

"That's it," Danny answered. He held up the piece of paper so that I could see it. "There's nothing else on the page. Come on, let's look for that book of spells you told me about."

We began searching the workshop for the big book I saw on Mr. Kronck's lap. I went through all the books in Mr. Kronck's book shelves. Danny opened desk drawers and file drawers.

"Nothing!" Danny exclaimed in frustration.

"Wait," I cautioned. "We haven't looked in this closet."

I opened a narrow closet door. Inside were more papers and old magazines—

And the book.

I recognized it right away. I picked up the old, brown, leather-bound volume with trembling fingers. "*The Book of Terror*," I read aloud. "That's what it's called."

I lifted the book out of the closet with both hands and carried it over to the table.

"Danny," I whispered. "This is it. *The Book of Terror* will tell us how to undo the curse!"

"Yes!" Danny ran his hand over the cover.

BANG! Something slammed behind us.

My stomach clenched. I whirled around.

I'd left the door to the workshop open.

But now it was shut. Bolted.

And right in front of it sat Mr. Kronck!

Chapter FIFTEEN

Oh, no!

We were trapped with the evil toymaker!

"What are you two doing in my workshop?" Mr. Kronck growled.

Danny and I stared in horror at him. His face was twisted with anger.

"Answer me!" he cried.

"We're—uh, we're looking for a b-b-book," Danny stammered.

I nodded. My throat was so dry I couldn't say a word.

"A book?" Mr. Kronck narrowed his eyes with suspicion.

"What kind of a book?"

"A book—like—like this one." Danny patted *The Book of Terror.* "An old book. Really old." He was babbling now. "Like more than fifty years old. You know, old books like this can be really valuable, and sometimes people don't know they've got these really valuable old books in—"

"Stop!" shouted Mr. Kronck. He glared at Danny. "Do you expect me to believe you sneaked in here in the middle of the night because you collect rare books?"

"Well . . ." Danny's face fell. "Not exactly."

"No! You've been spying on me!" Mr. Kronck turned to me. "Tell me why you're here," he demanded. "And tell me the truth!"

I'm not a good liar. I blurted out, "We know who you are, Mr. Kronck! We know what you do!"

Mr. Kronck's eyes opened a bit. "And what might that be?"

"You're the toymaker!" I was practically shouting now. "You make horrible toys that put curses on people! You have a headless doll. And a big long knife—I saw you waving it around! And you made a monkey that chokes little girls!"

"And Bess! What did you do with Bess?" Danny joined in.

"You put a curse on us," I accused Mr. Kronck. "We came here to find out how to break it!"

Mr. Kronck stared at us. Then he threw back

his head and made an awful, choking sound.

It took me a minute to realize what he was doing.

Mr. Kronck was laughing!

He laughed for a long time. Finally, his chuckles died down. He wiped his eyes.

"My goodness, you have a wild imagination!" he told me.

I stared at him in confusion.

"I'm not a toymaker," Mr. Kronck added.

He wasn't? "Then what are you?" I challenged.

He shrugged. "I'm a writer."

"A writer!" Danny and I both exclaimed.

Mr. Kronck nodded. "I write horror stories. I use this room to act out my scenes. If I write about a madman running around stabbing people, I have to know how it feels to be that madman. How it feels to stab someone."

I wished Mr. Kronck would stop talking about stabbing!

"I write mainly fiction," Mr. Kronck went on. "But for the last year, I've been working on a collection of legends from Fear Street."

"Legends from Fear Street!" Danny exclaimed. "You mean stuff that really happened here?"

Mr. Kronck nodded. "Some of my legends are taken from *The Book of Terror*. It was written long ago by one of the Fears."

"But why do you keep your work so secret?" I

asked. "Why did Mrs. Kronck stop us from coming in here the other night?"

"I've done all my research and writing in secret," Mr. Kronck explained. "This could be a best seller. And I don't want anyone else to get their hands on my stories."

I was starting to feel pretty foolish. I exchanged glances with Danny.

He still looked suspicious. "One more thing. What are you doing up in the middle of the night?" Danny demanded.

"I do my best work at night," Mr. Kronck told us. "So please—go home and leave me to it."

The old man spun his wheelchair around and opened the door for us. We apologized for sneaking into his workshop.

Then we left the Kroncks' house.

"So—do you buy that story?" I asked Danny as we walked back home. "You think he's really a writer?"

"I guess it makes sense," Danny admitted. "There were lots of books and papers in the workshop."

"Yeah, I guess. At least we got out of there alive," I added, opening the door to the kitchen.

I glanced at the kitchen clock. Twenty minutes to four!

We trudged upstairs. I was ready to drop.

As we passed Mom and Dad's room, I heard gentle snores coming from behind the closed door.

"I guess Bess is back from wherever she went," I whispered to Danny. "Should we wake her up?"

Danny shook his head. "We've got enough trouble already, without having to tell her we were outside in the middle of the night," he pointed out. "Let's talk to her tomorrow."

I started to nod. Then I froze as I caught sight of the far end of the hall. I felt the blood leave my cheeks.

There, in front of my door, sat the one-eyed blue monkey. His grin was pure evil.

I grabbed the horrible thing and shoved it into the closet.

Maybe Mr. Kronck wasn't the evil toymaker.

But the toymaker's curse was still with us.

I slept until almost noon on Sunday. Danny did, too.

When we finally stumbled downstairs, Bess was sitting at the kitchen table working on a word-search puzzle.

"Good morning, sleepyheads!" she greeted us. She looked fresh and rested. Her long gray hair was gathered up in a neat bun, and she was wearing a Kiss The Cook apron. "How about some waffles?"

"Yes, please!" I sat down at the table.

Bess got up to pour batter into the hot waffle iron.

"Bess, where were you last night?" Danny asked.

"We wanted to ask you something, but you weren't in Mom and Dad's room."

Bess laughed. "Oh, these old bones don't need much sleep," she told us. "I took a long walk around the neighborhood. The brisk night air always makes me feel good."

She put our waffles on plates and brought them over to us. "Sorry I wasn't around when you— Amanda!" she cried. "What have you done to your hand?"

My mouth was full of waffles. "She cut it," Danny answered for me. Then he told Bess about how we tried to get rid of the blue monkey. "We checked the rack on the grill," he finished. "And the monkey was gone. Burned to ashes. But when we came inside, and Amanda cut herself, the monkey was here! As if it never even got scorched!"

"That's awful!" Bess exclaimed. A worried frown came over her face. "I'm afraid it isn't a good sign."

Suddenly I didn't feel hungry anymore."What— what do you mean?" I asked.

"The monkey didn't burn," Bess told us. "Don't you see? The monkey didn't burn in the Fears' house fire, either." She shook her head slowly. "I'm afraid the story is repeating itself."

"No!" I cried. "Don't say that!"

Bess leaned forward. "The toymaker must be back on Fear Street," she told us. "There must be evil spells at work for the monkey to have so much power."

"But what can we do?" Danny practically shouted. "How can we break the curse?"

"There's only one thing you can do," Bess said urgently. "You must—"

She broke off suddenly.

I followed her gaze to the kitchen door.

I caught my breath.

The knob was turning slowly.

Slowly.

Then the door flew open.

Chapter SIXTEEN

"**S**urprise!" Dad called.

He and Mom burst into the kitchen.

I jumped up from the table and threw my arms around Dad and then Mom. I was so happy to see them!

"Our second workshop was cancelled," Mom said as I squeezed her tight. "So we came home a little early."

Dad laughed as Danny hugged him. "Well, this is quite a greeting," he said. "How were these kids, Bess?"

"They were perfect," Bess reported, smiling.

Finally, Danny and I let go of Mom and Dad.

"Are you packed up, Bess?" Dad asked. "I'll run you home now."

"It will take me two minutes to get my things together." Bess stood up from the table. "But don't worry about driving me home, Mr. Muller. I can walk."

Dad shook his head. "I wouldn't think of it," he said. "Not with your suitcase."

Bess hurried up to pack. "Thanks for everything," I told her when she came back down. "That chocolate chip cake was the best!"

Bess gave Danny a hug and then me. As she did, she whispered in my ear, "The toymaker is back, Amanda! Be very, very careful—or your whole family is doomed!"

A cold feeling spread through me. I shot a look at Danny. He was pale. Bess must have whispered the same words to him.

Then Dad took her suitcase and they walked out to the car.

"Well, I'm going upstairs to take a shower," Mom announced.

After she left the kitchen, I sat down at the table.

"There's only one thing to do," I announced. "We have to find this toymaker—before he destroys us."

Danny nodded somberly.

I raked my hands through my hair. "But how?" I moaned.

Danny grabbed a piece of paper and a pen from the counter. "We'll make a list of our chief suspects," he declared. "It could still be Mr. Kronck, I guess." He wrote "Mr. Kronck" on the list. "Who else?"

We racked our brains. But we couldn't come up with any other names.

"What are we going to do?" I wailed. "Mr. Kronck doesn't really seem evil. Just a little cranky. I don't have a clue how to find this stupid toymaker! Danny, maybe we should tell Mom and Dad about the monkey and the curse."

Danny snorted. "They'd never believe us," he said. "Plus, we couldn't tell them the whole story."

"True," I agreed gloomily. "Dad would *not* understand why I dug huge holes in his grass."

"Or why we broke into the Kroncks' house," Danny added. He frowned. "No. We keep the monkey a secret."

"But we have to protect Mom and Dad *somehow*," I protested. "You heard Bess. They could be in terrible danger!"

"We'll just have to follow them around and keep an eye on them," Danny decided. "Maybe we can stop the bad stuff from happening if we really look out for it."

It wasn't a very good plan. But it was the only one we had.

A few moments later we heard Dad's car pull up in the driveway. But he didn't come into the kitchen. I glanced out the kitchen window and saw him staring in dismay at the backyard.

"Uh-oh," Danny murmured. We headed outside.

"What in the world—?" Dad exclaimed as he surveyed the new damage to his precious lawn.

"Um—I forgot to tell you," I mumbled. "Omar says he's still working on your gopher problem."

Dad shook his head. "Well, he'd better find a solution soon. Look at those holes! This place is starting to look like a miniature golf course!" He bent and touched the grass. "And it's so dry. I think I'll get the hose out of the basement and give this lawn a good soaking." He started toward the house.

Get the hose out of the basement? The words rang in my ears.

The curse! Bess said one of the bad things that happened was that the little girl's father tripped over the blue monkey, fell down some stairs and broke his leg.

I gasped. If the story of the curse *was* repeating itself, that could happen to Dad!

We couldn't let him use the stairs!

"No!" I cried, dashing after Dad. "Don't go down there!"

He halted and stared at me curiously. "Why on earth not?"

"Uh—I mean, let Danny and me get the hose for you," I stammered. "You must be tired from all that driving."

Dad gave a puzzled laugh. "Well, I'm not exactly a doddering old geezer, but—all right, Amanda. If you want to get the hose for me, be my guest. Thanks."

"No problem." I grabbed Danny's arm and towed him into the kitchen.

"What is this?" Danny demanded, tugging his arm free. "You get the dumb hose, since you volunteered."

"Come on! I'm protecting Dad," I whispered.

That got his attention. As we went down the basement steps, I explained my theory. When I was done, he nodded.

"You're right," Danny admitted. "And there are other things we have to watch out for too. What else happened in the story?"

I thought. "Well, the family dog choked on the monkey's arm and died," I remembered.

"No problem. We don't have a dog," Danny pointed out.

I unhooked the hose from its hook on the wall. "And the house burned down," I added.

"Right." Danny nodded. "We better make sure Mom and Dad don't light any fires."

All afternoon and into the evening, Danny and I followed Mom and Dad around. We tried to make sure Dad didn't go up or down any stairs, and that neither of them lit any matches or anything. Lucky for us we have an electric stove!

The whole time, I kept waiting for bad luck to strike.

But nothing happened.

After dinner that night, Danny and I sat with Mom and Dad in the living room—something we never do. They read. I stared at the TV, not really knowing what I was watching. My mind churned.

How could we find the toymaker?

Dad stood up. "Anybody want anything from the kitchen?"

No one did. Dad walked into the hall, flicking the switch for the overhead light as he went.

"Hmm. Bulb's burnt out," I heard him mutter. His footsteps clicked down the hall. "Guess I might as well get the ladder and change it right now."

Get the ladder?

Danny and I both realized what Dad was doing at the same moment. We stared at each other in horror.

But before we could even move—

THUD, THUD, THUD, THUD!

Then a horrible scream filled the air.

Chapter SEVENTEEN

Mom jumped up, looking alarmed. "What in the world—?"

"Dad!" I cried.

We all rushed to the top of the basement stairs.

Dad lay at the bottom of the steps, clutching his leg.

"My leg!" he moaned. "I think it's broken!"

Mom gasped and hurried down to him. She put her hand on Dad's injured leg. He groaned.

"We have to get you to the hospital," Mom announced. "I'm going upstairs to call an ambulance."

Mom ran up to the phone.

Danny and I hurried down to Dad. I took one of his hands. Danny held the other. I could tell from his face that he was in terrible pain.

"The ambulance will be here any minute," I assured him.

Dad closed his eyes and nodded.

That's when I noticed what was on the bottom step.

Right next to Dad's injured leg.

The blue monkey.

Its one eye glowed a bright, evil red.

You're doomed! it seemed to say. *You're all doomed!*

The ambulance showed up a few moments later. Two paramedics lifted Dad onto a stretcher and carried him outside.

"I called Bess," Mom told us as she fished her car keys out of her purse. "She's coming over to stay with you. She has a key. I'll call you from the hospital!"

Then Mom jumped into her car and took off after the ambulance.

Danny and I stared at each other.

"You know what we have to do," he said.

I nodded. "We have to get the blue monkey and keep it with us—so it can't slip off and make more bad luck."

"Right," Danny agreed.

But it took us a long, long time to get up enough courage to go down in the basement to get the horrible toy.

At last we went down together. I picked up the monkey and we ran back upstairs.

"We're not letting you out of our sight again," I told it. Then I turned to Danny. "Where shall we put it?"

"Let's tie it to one of the heavy chairs in the living room so it can't get away," he suggested. "I'll get some rope."

As he came back from the garage, the phone rang. Danny and I both raced to get it. I won.

"Hi, honey," Mom's voice came over the line. "I'm at the hospital. The doctors have set Dad's leg, and now they're putting a cast on it."

"Does putting a cast on hurt?" I asked.

"No, the worst part is over," Mom assured me. "And don't worry. In a few weeks, Dad is going to be as good as new."

I swallowed hard. "When are you coming home?"

"Not for a while." Mom paused. "Is Bess there?"

"Not yet," I answered.

"Don't worry," Mom said. "She'll be there soon."

Tears sprang to my eyes. "Hurry home, Mom."

"We'll be home before you know it, honey. Oh, by the way, we brought Bess a thank-you gift. She left in such a hurry earlier that I didn't get the chance to give it to her. It's in the bottom of my suitcase. Will you take it out and put it on my bed so that I'll remember to give it to her later?"

"Sure, Mom," I promised absently.

I hung up and told Danny what Mom said about Dad's leg.

"That's good," Danny said. "Okay, let's go tie up this monkey."

We headed down the hall to the living room. I was about to hand the monkey to Danny when I heard the sound.

Tap, tap.

Still holding the monkey, I turned and stared at the window. It was pitch dark.

Except for a pale face.

Omar!

He was so creepy!

"What does that weirdo want now?" Danny complained.

We stepped closer. Omar was motioning to us when his gaze fell on the monkey in my hands. And his face changed completely.

His one eye bulged.

His skin flushed an ugly, dark color.

His mouth twisted into an evil grimace.

"Give me that monkey!" Omar bellowed.

Chapter EIGHTEEN

"The monkey!" Omar yelled. "Give it to me!"

That's when the horrible truth hit me.

"Danny!" I screamed. *"Omar is the toymaker!"*

Omar leered at us. Then he disappeared from the window.

"He's going to the front door!" I cried. "Quick! We have to lock him out!"

Danny and I raced for the door.

As we ran, I wondered why we hadn't figured this out before.

Omar was old and creepy.

He lurked around our house at all hours of the night.

He seemed to appear out of nowhere, like a magician.

An evil magician!

We reached the door just as Omar was pushing it open. I slammed it in his face. Danny flipped the lock.

"Give me the monkey!" Omar yelled through the door. "You don't know what's going on here!"

"We know who you are!" I shouted back. "And we're not giving you the monkey!"

"Right!" Danny shouted. "So go away!"

We waited for Omar's reply.

But we didn't hear anything.

Suddenly I realized what he was doing.

"The back door!" I shouted. "He's headed for the back door!"

Danny and I raced to the kitchen.

The knob on the door to the garage was already turning!

Danny and I hit the door at the same time. We pushed it shut. I double bolted it.

I leaned my back against it, panting. Danny plopped down in a kitchen chair.

And we waited for Omar's next move.

We didn't have to wait long.

BAM! BAM! BAM!

Omar pounded the door with his fist. I could feel the wood shudder against my back.

"You must give me the monkey!" he yelled. "I must have it!"

"Amanda," Danny whispered, "Maybe we should just give it to him. Maybe then he'll go away and we'll be rid of it."

"But he's the toymaker!" I whispered back. "He's evil! Why does he want the monkey so badly? It must be so he can do awful things with it! Like kill our whole family!"

BAM! BAM! BAM!

I clutched the monkey tightly. No way was I letting Omar get his hands on it! I pressed my back against the door.

"Well, we found the toymaker. But—what do we do with him?" I wailed.

"Shhhh!" Danny put a finger to his lips. "What's that?"

I listened.

I didn't hear a thing.

"What did you hear?" I asked Danny.

"I'm not sure," he said.

It was quiet. Too quiet.

"What do you think Omar is up to?" I whispered.

"Who knows?" Danny put his ear against the door. "I don't hear him out there."

I pressed my ear against the door too. Silence.

Danny nudged me. "Amanda, I think he's gone!"

"Not really," a deep voice growled from behind us.

Chapter NINETEEN

Danny and I whirled.

My heart went THUD.

Omar stood in the kitchen doorway. He leered at us with his lone blue eye.

How did he get into the house?

It didn't matter, really. Because here he was.

He held out a grimy hand.

"Give me the blue monkey," he demanded. "Before it's too late!"

I thrust the monkey behind my back.

"No!" I cried. "You'll only use it to hurt us!"

Omar shook his head. "I would never do that," he said.

Yeah, sure.

Omar began walking slowly toward me with his hand held out. "Please," he said softly, "give it to me."

I shot a glance at Danny.

He gave me a small nod.

I knew we were thinking the same thing.

We waited until Omar was right in front of us. Then we took off! I ran around one side of him, while Danny ran around the other side.

Omar reached out to grab me. But I dodged away.

Danny was already speeding down the hall. I followed.

Omar tore after us. "Come back here!" he bellowed.

As Danny and I raced for the front door, we nearly crashed into someone coming in. Bess!

"Bess!" I cried. I threw my arms around her.

We were saved!

But Bess didn't hug me back. Instead, she stared straight ahead.

Stared at Omar.

Omar glared back at her with his steely blue eye. Danny and I seemed caught between the two of them.

"So we meet again," Omar growled, glaring at Bess.

"He's the toymaker!" I shouted to Bess. "It's him!"

"Leave these children alone!" Bess shouted at Omar. She put one arm around me and one around Danny.

Omar shook his head. "Don't listen to her, kids," he warned. "*She's* the one who started all this trouble."

Once more he held out a hand. "Give me the monkey," he begged. "And all your troubles will be over."

I wished I could fling the horrible blue monkey at Omar. Then I would be rid of the thing!

But I couldn't do that. I couldn't hand the monkey over to the toymaker!

"Why are you blaming Bess?" Danny yelled at Omar.

"Bess? Her name isn't Bess," Omar retorted. "At least it wasn't when I knew her. Then her name was Olga." He stared at Danny, then at me. "Olga the Toymaker."

"WHAT?" I cried. "You're saying that *Bess* is the toymaker?"

Omar nodded. "That's right. And she's evil, through and through."

"Don't listen to him!" Bess snapped. Her voice was hard. "He'll say anything to get that monkey."

Omar fixed his one eye on me. "Give me the blue monkey," he urged. "And I'll prove that she's the toymaker."

"Don't do it, Amanda!" Bess whispered in my ear. "Don't give it to him!"

I felt so confused! I broke away from Bess's grasp. So did Danny.

We stood gazing from Bess's face to Omar's.

We had to choose sides with one of them.

But which one was telling the truth?

Chapter TWENTY

Omar cleared his throat. "It happened fifty years ago today," he rumbled, staring at Bess. He seemed to have forgotten that Danny and I were there.

Bess nodded. "Exactly," she agreed.

"*What* happened fifty years ago today?" Danny demanded.

"The house burned to the ground," Omar's voice was low. "It happened in this spot. Where your house is now. Right here."

"Stop it, Omar!" Bess cried. "Don't you threaten to burn down this house! Don't you dare!"

That was when I knew I had to trust Bess. She was the one who looked out for us. Who would always be there to protect us.

"Here!" I thrust the blue monkey into Bess's arms.

A smile spread over her face as she took the toy.

"Get out of here, Omar!" I shouted. "Get away from this house! And don't come back!"

Omar glowered at us.

"You've made a bad mistake," he snarled. "I only hope you live long enough to regret it."

"Go away!" Danny shouted. "Before we call the police!"

"Right!" Bess chimed in. "You tell him, Danny!"

"I'll go," Omar growled at last. "But I'll be around." He leaned toward me. "I'll be watching," he added.

Omar shoved past us to the open front door. He strode out and vanished into the darkness.

"We better follow him," Danny said grimly. "Make sure he really leaves."

"Right. Don't let him set fire to *your* house!" Bess urged.

Our house! No! We couldn't let the toymaker burn it down!

Danny and I raced out into the night. We ran around to the backyard.

I spotted Omar stooping by the garden shed.

He had something in his hand.

My heart nearly stopped when I saw what it was.

A box of matches!

"Stop him, Danny!" I cried. "Before he burns down the house!"

Danny grabbed a shovel that Omar had left leaning against a tree. "Go away!" Danny shouted. He held the shovel blade up, waving it menacingly at Omar.

Omar stared at us for a moment. In the shadows, I couldn't read the expression on his face.

Then he tossed the match box at us.

"You're doomed now," he murmured. His voice sounded tired. "It's just a matter of time."

"Noooo!" Danny took off after Omar, waving the shovel.

Omar merely put up a hand, as if saying, "Enough." Then he turned and jogged off into the dark.

Danny let the shovel fall from his hand. He stood by the fence, trying to catch his breath.

"Nice work," I told him.

"He's gone," Danny panted. "And now we know the truth. The whole time, the toymaker was right in our own backyard."

We turned back to the house. Bess stood outside the garage. Her long gray skirt fluttered in the breeze as she watched us walk toward her.

"You did the right thing," Bess said. With one hand, she held open the back door so that Danny and I could come inside. With the other, she held the blue monkey.

I plopped down into a chair at the kitchen table.

"So are you going to keep that monkey?" I asked, shuddering.

Bess simply smiled. "How about some brownies before you go to bed?" she offered. "I baked them when I was home. I put chocolate chips in them."

"Sounds great!" I answered, grinning.

"Yeah." Danny leaned against the fridge.

Bess walked over to the counter. "Two brownies, coming right up." She began peeling the plastic wrap off the baking dish.

I propped my chin in my hands. Suddenly I felt very tired.

"I can't believe Omar said *you* were the toymaker, Bess," I scoffed. "Is that ridiculous or what?"

Bess didn't answer. She just kept cutting the brownies. Then she turned and carried them over to the table.

"The thing about Omar," Bess remarked thoughtfully as she set the brownies down in front of us, "is that he was right."

"What?" Danny exclaimed.

I stared at Bess. "Right about what?"

She smiled down at us.

"Right about me," she said. "You see, *I am the toymaker.*"

Chapter TWENTY-ONE

I felt as though my heart had stopped beating.

Bess? The toymaker?

"No jokes!" Danny wailed. "Not after the night we've had!"

"It's not a joke." Bess smiled. But it wasn't her usual pleasant smile.

It was the same hideous grin that was on the face of the blue monkey!

Every hair on my arms and legs stood straight up.

Bess sat down at the table with us.

"Eat," she said. "There's nothing wrong with the brownies."

Maybe not. But suddenly I wasn't hungry. Danny wasn't digging into his brownie, either.

"I thought your gardener looked familiar," Bess told us. She fluffed the monkey's blue fur. "But I hadn't seen Omar for so many years. Not since the night of the fire. You see, Omar is part of the Fear family. He's the older brother of the little girl in the story."

"Omar?" I gasped.

Bess nodded. "His hair used to be red," she murmured, smiling. "Just like yours."

I noticed that her eyes had taken on a glow. A reddish glow.

"I've waited a long time to make my comeback," she told us. "Half a century—just waiting for the right time."

"You planned this?" Danny sputtered. "You planned for us to dig up the monkey?"

Bess nodded. "I wanted to see my greatest creation again." She ran a wrinkled hand over the blue monkey. "It's the most amazing toy in the world. I knew it was buried in your yard, but I didn't know where. So—the easiest way to get it was to have you dig it up for me. I knew if I told you the story of the curse, it would be only a matter of time before you dug it up."

"But I thought you liked us!" I cried. "Why do you want to put a curse on our family?"

Bess shrugged. "Your family moved into a house on this cursed spot. That was your bad luck.

Nothing good will ever happen in this place. Not while I'm around!"

Bess paused, rubbing her hands together as if she was warming them up. "I didn't start all this, you know," she went on after a moment. "No, it was that little girl. When she stole the blue monkey, she set things rolling. She brought the curse down upon this place. And now you have to pay for her mistake!" Bess laughed—a hard, evil laugh. "Now your family is doomed. Doomed by the power of my monkey!"

I glared at Bess. How could she have pretended to care for us? She put her arms around us—and it was all so she could bring us to our doom!

I wanted to stand up and shove the table over on her!

"Wait a second," Danny objected. "You told us the curse wouldn't work unless someone accepted the monkey as a gift. Amanda and I dug up the monkey."

Bess's laugh echoed through the kitchen. "That's right!" she screamed. "That's the best part of *this* story! When you brought the monkey to me, you gave me the perfect opportunity."

"H-how?" I asked, even though I wasn't sure I wanted to hear the answer.

"You set the monkey down on the table," Bess reminded us. "That's when I told you it had to be a gift. Remember? I picked it up and said, 'This is a gift,' and handed it to you."

I did remember! How could I have been so stupid?

"You're evil!" I said between clenched teeth. "You think you're so great because you tricked us—a couple of kids who trusted you! But you're just plain evil."

"I am evil," Bess agreed. She sounded proud of it! "I am more evil than you can imagine. But I'm going to make sure you don't have to *imagine* anything!"

Bess leaped up and began pacing the room. "You'll see!" she ranted. "You won't know what hit you!"

Danny's hand inched toward the knife rack. He reached up and grasped a long, glittering blade.

"I don't think that's a very good idea," Bess snapped, never even glancing at Danny. Her voice was calm and cold. "If you try to hurt me in any way, I'll put a curse on you that's ten times more powerful than the one you're living with now!"

Danny swallowed. Then he lowered the knife.

"And you'd better not tell anyone my little secret," Bess warned. "Not your parents. Not anyone! If you do, you'll regret it for the rest of your very short life. Now get upstairs, you brats. I don't feel like looking at you any longer."

Danny and I went. We didn't dare disobey.

As we were filing out of the kitchen, Bess snatched up the blue monkey. She thrust it into my hands.

"Don't forget your toy!" she cackled. "Now play nicely, children!"

"We're doomed!" Danny moaned. "There's no way out of this!"

"Don't say that," I told him.

We were huddled in my bedroom. With the blue monkey.

I set it on my pillow. Maybe if I put it in its favorite spot, it would stop making bad things happen for a while.

I was perched on the foot of my bed. Danny sat at my desk.

Bess was downstairs. I didn't know what she was doing. I didn't want to know.

I just hoped it had nothing to do with matches!

"We'll come up with something," I told Danny. "It's too horrible to think of living with this curse on us forever."

Forever—or until the house caught on fire with us locked in the bedroom.

Danny gnawed on his thumb. "According to Bess—or Olga, or whatever her name is—there's one way to get rid of the curse. We have to pass the monkey on to someone else. As a gift."

I shuddered. "There's got to be another way. Can you think of anyone you hate enough to put *this* curse on them?"

"If only we could give the monkey to Bess!" Danny exclaimed. "That would solve our problems. But there's no chance she'd ever take it from us." He sighed. "Face it, Amanda. We're toast!"

I sat up straight. I was starting to get an idea.

"Maybe not, Danny," I said slowly. "I have a plan."

Chapter TWENTY-TWO

It was almost eleven when the knob turned on my bedroom door.

Bess stuck her head in. "You can come out now," she told us. "I just got a call from your parents. They're on their way home."

"Yes!" Danny jumped up.

"Remember, children," Bess added. "Not a word about our little secret to anyone. Or else!" She slid her index finger across her throat.

I stared at her evil face and wondered how I ever could have thought she looked kind.

Danny and I walked obediently down the stairs. Bess followed behind us. A moment later Mom's car pulled into the driveway.

Danny and I ran out to greet Mom and Dad.

"Dad!" I cried. "How are you? How's your leg?"

"Getting better all the time," Dad promised. He swung his leg out of the car. "But get your magic markers out, kids. I'm counting on you to do something about this boring white cast."

Dad climbed slowly out of the car. He hobbled up the front path on a pair of wooden crutches. Mom stayed at his side, murmuring encouragement.

"I'm so sorry about your leg, Mr. Muller," Bess told Dad as he hopped into the house. "That must have been a nasty fall."

Dad grimaced. "It was," he agreed. "Talk about bad luck!"

Bess clicked her tongue against the roof of her mouth. "Bad luck is so nasty. You never know when it's going to hit you."

Danny and I exchanged glances. What a phony!

In the kitchen, Mom grasped Bess's arm. "Bess," she gushed. "I can't thank you enough for coming over here again to look after Amanda and Danny— especially on such short notice! I felt so good knowing that they were in your hands."

Bess smiled. "Oh, it was my pleasure, Mrs. Muller."

Dad struggled into the living room. Danny took his crutches while I helped him put his broken leg up on the sofa.

"You win the most devoted sitter of the year

award, Bess," Dad declared as Bess and Mom came into the living room. "I don't know what we would have done without you this weekend."

I knew. But I also knew better than to say anything that would make Bess angry.

"Well, if you folks are set, I'll be leaving," Bess told Mom and Dad. She turned towards Danny and me. I saw a glimmer of red flash from her eyes. "Don't worry, kids," she added. "I'll be back soon."

"Anytime, Bess," Mom said warmly. "We always love to have you here."

I felt like gagging. But I pasted a smile on my face.

Mom, Danny and I followed Bess into the front hall. She picked up her purse from a chair. "I hope you enjoy the rest of your evening." She glanced at me and Danny with a little smile. "I'll be thinking of you."

Mom suddenly snapped her fingers. "Oh, hold on a minute. I almost forgot!" She raced upstairs. "Don't go anywhere, Bess!" she called over her shoulder.

A moment later, Mom came back down. In her hands she held a gift-wrapped package. She passed it to Bess. "We picked this up for you in Scottsboro. Just a little gift."

"Why, thank you!" Bess looked pleased.

"Open it!" Mom urged. "I hope you'll like it."

Bess untied the bright blue bow and slowly unwrapped the flowered paper that covered the box. She set the paper on the hall table. Carefully, she lifted the lid of the box.

I held my breath as she stared into the box.

And then—

"No!" Bess screamed. "No!"

Inside the box lay the blue monkey.

It stared up at Bess, its one evil eye glowing.

I couldn't keep a grin off my face. While we waited for Mom and Dad to come home, Danny and I had replaced Mom and Dad's present with the blue monkey! I spent a long time rewrapping the gift so no one could tell I'd opened it.

Mom's eyes widened. "What's wrong, Bess?" she asked. "Don't you like it? I thought it was such a lovely pottery bowl."

Bess only glared at Danny and me. She didn't even seem to hear Mom's words.

"Well, Bess," Danny taunted. "Do you like it?"

"No!" Bess shrieked. "You can't curse me with my own magic!"

"Too late!" I shouted. "We already did!"

Mom's jaw was practically to the floor. "Amanda! Danny!" she cried. "What's going on?"

"Yeah!" Dad called from the living room. "What's going on?"

Bess hurled the monkey to the floor. "You two will regret this!" she snarled. "You think you've beaten me at my own game? Ha! Think again!"

Mom's eyes grew wide with amazement. "Bess, really!"

"Hey!" Dad called again. "Will somebody tell me what's going on?"

Fuming, Bess yanked open the front door.

As she did, a gusty breeze swirled into the house. Bess's long gray skirt floated out in back of her as she struggled to get out the door against the wind.

The wind picked up the toy monkey and whisked it out the door. The monkey's long blue arms reached out toward the hem of Bess's skirt. Its little hands clapped shut on the gray fabric.

But Bess never noticed. She hurried down the front path, unaware that the blue monkey—her own greatest creation—was clinging tightly to her.

The blue monkey was hers now. And so was its curse.

I shook my head as I watched her go, the monkey clamped to her skirt.

The perfect gift.

And she didn't even say thank you!

Are you ready to meet aliens in Shadyside?
Turn the page for a sneak preview of the first chapter of
I Was a Sixth-Grade Zombie

I WAS A SIXTH-GRADE
ZOMBIE

Coming in May 1998

"I don't get it," I said to my best friend, Mark. I gazed around my empty basement. "This is supposed to be the best show yet. It's got albino worm creatures as big as humans! Where *is* everybody?"

On Wednesday afternoons after school my basement fills with kids. They come to watch my favorite TV show of all time, *Strange Cases*. It's about two investigators for a secret agency. They check out weird paranormal stuff.

It usually turns out to be even weirder than they think.

Strange Cases actually runs at ten o'clock on Tuesday nights. Most of us are in bed by then. Or at least we're not allowed to be watching TV that late. So I tape it and show it Wednesday afternoons on my VCR.

We have a great time watching it. We munch on microwave popcorn. We rewind and look at the weirdest stuff in slo-mo. We argue about whether it could ever really happen.

I kind of think it could. See, I live on Fear Street, in the town of Shadyside. Weird things happen on Fear Street. Creepy things. People say they've seen ghosts there—and worse.

I've never seen anything weird. But I'm still hoping.

Mark and I haven't told anyone, but we want to be investigators when we grow up.

Anyway, when we watch *Strange Cases*, we all have lots to talk about.

But last week only three people besides Mark showed up.

This week Mark and I were the only ones here.

What was going on?

Mark took a gulp of cream soda. He loves that stuff. Gross!

"Come on, Valerie," he urged. "Let's start the tape."

"But, Mark, where *is* everybody?"

Mark stuffed a handful of popcorn in his mouth before he answered. He's always hungry.

Mark is one of the shortest boys in our sixth grade class. I'm one of the tallest girls. We've been best friends since third grade, when we were both the same size.

Mark has short black hair, dark tan skin, and a space between his front teeth. He wears wire-rimmed glasses. And he's very quiet.

I have strawberry-blond hair and freckles. And a big mouth. I'm the opposite of Mark. Maybe that's why we're such good friends.

"Mph phmbf mmph," Mark said.

I poked him. "What?"

Mark swallowed. "Let's phone them."

I grabbed the phone and dialed AJ Hilton's number.

"Who are you?" AJ's little brother, Bart, screamed over the phone.

I held the receiver away from my ear. "A friend of AJ's," I hollered back. No one can outscream me! "Where is he?"

"Ow, my ear! At his dumb club!" Bart slammed the phone down.

I told Mark what Bart said. "What club?" he asked.

"I don't know. I thought *this* was our club. The *Strange Cases* Club," I answered, frowning.

Weird.

We tried Elaine Costello's number next. Her mom answered. "Oh, of course, Valerie," she said. "Elaine joined the M-W Club. Aren't you in it?"

"Uh—no," I told her. I hung up, puzzled. "Have you ever heard of the M-W Club?" I asked Mark.

"Don't you remember? The afterschool clubs Mr. Hool started. The Monday-Wednesday Club and the Tuesday-Thursday Club. He called them M-W and Two Ts."

"Oh, yeah," I muttered. "*Those* clubs. The loser clubs."

Mr. Hool was new. He started teaching at Shadyside Middle School after winter break. He wore thick diamond-shaped glasses that made his pale eyes look twice as big as normal. He was super-tall, too.

And he was always cold. In winter he walked around in three sweaters and a jacket—inside the school building! Now that spring was here, he cut back to two layers.

He had lots of ideas, including this one about the clubs. "Each one of you should join a club," Mr. Hool told us on his first day. "Maximize your brain power! Strengthen your bodies! Polish your manners! Become the best children you can be!"

I decided right then that this guy was a major weirdo. The clubs sounded *so* lame. Mark and I didn't even consider joining. As usual, we were in total agreement.

So how come everyone else joined?

How could kids pass up *Strange Cases* for some dumb club?

"Come on, Val," Mark said again. "If those guys want to miss *Strange Cases*, that's their problem. Start the tape."

"Wait. Let's try Steve Hickock first," I suggested. "He'd never join one of those clubs. He's way too cool."

Mark riffled through the phone book until he found the number. I dialed. Steve's mom picked up.

"Hi, Valerie," she said in a distracted voice. Steve's baby sister, Gretchen, wailed in the background. "Steve isn't home. He's off at some club."

I couldn't believe it! Steve too? How come our friends joined this dumb club and never even told me and Mark?

"Do you know where the club is?" I asked Steve's mom.

"On Oak Street, just past the bowling alley," she replied.

"Thanks." I put the phone down and made up my mind.

"Let's go check out this club," I said to Mark.

He stared sadly at the VCR for a minute. Then he nodded.

"Where did that come from?" Mark asked.

"I don't know. I never noticed it before." I stared at the big pale-blue building on Oak Street. "How could I miss it?"

It was slick, almost see-through—but not quite. It looked like a giant ice cube. I shivered just looking at it. There was only one window—a tiny dark square right next to a pale yellow door. A uniformed guard sat scowling behind the glass.

As we watched, three kids marched up the sidewalk. One of them was Ginger Park. She smart-mouthed Mr. Hool in class that day. The other two pulled a fire alarm.

"Weren't they all given detention after school?" Mark asked.

I checked my watch. School let out half an hour ago.

"Maybe they got sent to the clubs instead of detention," Mark suggested.

I snorted. "Yeah. The clubs are so boring, they're worse punishment."

The kids stepped up to the yellow door. They unzipped their backpacks and took out what looked like credit cards.

One by one they stuck the cards into a slot on the door. A buzz sounded and the door opened for each kid.

"What do they *do* in there?" Mark wondered.

"Let's find out!" We crossed the street and approached the guard's window.

"Hi." I smiled. "Can we go inside?"

The guard frowned. "Your key cards are where?"

Key cards? He must mean those things the other kids used to open the door. "Uh—I forgot mine," I lied.

The guard glared at me. "No card, no entry."

I usually don't give up that easily. But for some reason I couldn't think of any arguments. I stared at the guard.

Luckily Mark tugged my arm and pulled me away.

Mark and I make a good team. When I'm brain-dead, he kicks into action. And vice versa.

We ducked around the corner. On this side the

building was a flat blue wall two stories tall and a block wide. There wasn't a single window.

Mark's eyes were narrow. "It's sure got a lot of security for an after-school club." He reached toward the slick blue wall.

Before Mark's fingers actually touched the wall, his hand slipped sideways. "Whoa!" he exclaimed, and tried it again.

Again his hand slipped before he could touch the surface.

Mark's eyes grew perfectly round. He turned and stared at me. "Val," he whispered. "I think that's a force field!"

"A *force field*?" The hair on the back of my neck prickled. "That's impossible!" I sputtered.

Force fields don't exist in *real* life, I thought. Only in sci-fi movies. Or TV programs like *Strange Cases*.

Mark grabbed my hand and pulled it toward the building. My hand was pushed away from the blue wall. By something invisible.

Mark was right. We were inches away from a strong force field.

We had just found our very own strange case.

About R.L. Stine

R.L. Stine is the best-selling author in America. He has written more than one hundred scary books for young people, all of them bestsellers.

His series include *Fear Street, Ghosts of Fear Street,* and the *Fear Street Sagas*.

Bob grew up in Columbus, Ohio. Today he lives in New York City with his wife, Jane, his son, Matt, and his dog, Nadine.

Don't Miss

R.L.Stine's
Ghosts of Fear Street #30

I WAS A SIXTH-GRADE ZOMBIE

Valerie and Mark know something is strange about the new after-school clubs. They are held in a weird building surrounded by a force field. And none of the kids who joined the clubs can ever remember what happens in them. But when Valerie and Mark decide to check it out, they find more terror than they bargained for. It seems Val and Mark have joined their own special club—and someone is controlling every move they make!